THEODORE NASH

The Vampire Killer

Ashley Carvel

To my wife —
lover of clever mysteries and even cleverer banter,
who somehow fell for a man who can't stop making
inappropriate jokes at the wrong time and writing strange
books.
You've been my rock, my reason, my forever.
Two kids, one home, endless cups of tea, and one very lucky
husband.
I wrote this for you. And I'd do it all again.

CONTENTS

INTRODUCTION

Every town has its shadows.

In 1943 East Hounslow, those shadows belonged to a killer.

Not a monster out of stories. Not some creature with fangs and myth behind it. No, this was something colder. Smarter. Human.

They called him The Vampire Killer.

A name born from rumour, from ritual. Victims drained, their lives measured and displayed with deliberate care. Six bodies. No clear motive. No connection. No mistakes.

And when the war-weary streets started whispering about monsters, the kind that wore a man's face , someone had to listen.

Enter Theodore Nash. A mind sharper than most, quieter than some would like, and not nearly as detached as he pretends to be.

This isn't a story about vampires.

It's about patterns, obsession, and the cost of chasing truth when the shadows run deeper than anyone dares admit.

THE VAMPIRE KILLER

1. A HOUSE OF STILLNESS

21:22 07/03/1943
12 Bridge Road, East Hounslow

Theodore Nash stepped out of the police car, his polished shoes pressing into the damp cobblestone street. The cold bite of the night air settled into his coat as he took in the scene before him, a two-story house, its exterior modest but well-kept, standing at the very edge of the village. The front door was slightly ajar, an eerie invitation into silence.

A police lantern flickered against the gloom, casting long, twisted shadows onto the pavement. The street beyond was empty. Curtains in neighbouring houses remained drawn, their inhabitants choosing ignorance over curiosity. The villagers here had learned, long before tonight, that when death came knocking, it was best not to listen.

Detective Inspector James Radcliffe stood at the threshold, adjusting his coat against the chill. His expression, as always, was unreadable, stone-faced, yet carrying the weight of someone who had seen far too many of these scenes. He was broad-shouldered, silver threading his temples, and his presence carried the kind of authority that rarely required words.

Standing a few steps behind him, Detective Wallace Tucton struck a match against his shoe, lighting a cigarette with the ease of a man who treated murder scenes like casual inconveniences. His hair was dishevelled, his tie loosened, and his mouth was curled into what could only be described as an amused smirk.

"You took your time," Radcliffe muttered, eyes flicking toward Theo.

Theo took a measured breath, adjusting his gloves. "Time is relative."

Tucton let out a short bark of laughter. "Ah, classic Nash. Just arrived and already sounding like an insufferable prick."

Theo ignored him, stepping past both men into the house.

The moment he crossed the threshold, the air thickened, heavy with the scent of copper and something almost sickly sweet. The dim light from the street barely penetrated the gloom, leaving long shadows stretching across the walls.

The silence was near absolute, broken only by the distant metronome ticking of a clock. The house wasn't abandoned, nor was it in disarray. No overturned furniture, no signs of forced entry. Everything remained precisely where it should be, except for the body in the centre of the room.

It hung from the wooden beam above, upside down, ankles bound by thick, meticulously tied rope. The victim's throat was slashed clean across, the wound so precise it almost looked surgical. Blood had flowed freely, forming a perfectly symmetrical circle on the floor beneath.

Theo tilted his head slightly, taking in the scene like a painter admiring the strokes of a masterpiece. There was something deeply intentional about the way the body had been displayed. No chaos, no excess. Whoever had done this had experience.

Radcliffe exhaled through his nose. "It's getting worse."

"Worse?" Theo murmured, stepping closer.

Tucton exhaled a cloud of smoke from the doorway.

"Six bodies in. Same ritual, same precision, same eerie lack of struggle. And yet we still don't have a single fucking clue who's doing it."

Theo's eyes flicked toward him. "You sound impressed."

Tucton smirked. "Oh, I'm deeply disturbed, but credit where credit's due, this bastard's consistent."

Radcliffe shot him a look but said nothing. Instead, his attention returned to Theo. "What do you see?"

Theo didn't answer immediately. He let his mind settle into the scene, taking in each meticulous detail.

There was no sense of struggle here. The victim hadn't fought back. Either he had been unconscious at the time of the killing... or he had trusted his killer enough not to run. The rope had been tied with a constrictor knot, clean, centred, and pulled taut with symmetrical precision. It wasn't a common knot for everyday use. It was used in professions that demanded secure bindings: arborists, surgeons, butchers. People who understood tension and balance, who knew how to control weight. Not a sailor's knot. Not improvised. Practiced. Deliberate.

Theo crouched slightly, his eyes trailing the fibres of the rope, tracing its placement around the ankles, noting the pressure lines against the skin. There was no chafing. No bruising. The victim had been tied post-mortem or close enough to it. Death first. Positioning after.

He glanced at the ceiling beam. Notched. Not splintered. The hook had already been there, screwed in with a hand far more careful than any burglar or brute. Someone had prepared this. Not hours before. Days. Maybe weeks. A home visited once, scouted, mapped.

He pulled out some surgical gloves and fitted them as he walked the perimeter of the circle of blood, three feet in diameter. A precise number. Measured, not estimated. Poured from a container, in this case a body, rather than spattered from struggle. There was purpose in the pour. The symmetry was not an accident. It never was.

He ran a gloved finger along the groove between floorboards, lifting the faintest smear of residue, sawdust. Recent. Barely settled. Someone had filed or sanded something in this room.

That didn't align with the victim.

His shoes. Loafers, polished. A man who wore cologne, who drank filtered water and wiped his glasses even when they weren't dirty. A detail-oriented man. He would not have tolerated that layer of dust. The sawdust belonged to the killer.

Theo stepped back, tilting his head toward the fireplace. No scent of ash. No warmth. Cold for hours, maybe since morning. A thin layer of soot on the hearthstone had been disturbed in a crescent shape, someone had stepped there and wiped it clean. Perhaps instinctively. Perhaps to hide something.

The glass on the side table caught the low light. Theo moved to it. Water line still distinct. Half full. Or half empty. Depending on how long it had been since the last sip. The angle of the glass on the coaster was just a touch off-centre. The rim faced the far end of the couch, not the body. A guest's placement.

He paused. A guest.

He turned to the couch, noting the cushions. One was slightly compressed. Not by the victim, too narrow a frame. Smaller weight. The indent was recent. Gravity hadn't had time to restore the shape. Female, perhaps. Or a slight man.

Theo's stomach shifted. Not discomfort. Not fear. A familiar chill. The kind that comes before revelation.

And then, there it was.

The object resting on the mantelpiece.

A cube, smooth and clear, catching the light in a way that almost made it glow. Inside, frozen in time, was a swirl of dark red.

Theo stepped forward, picking it up carefully. Turning it over in his palm. The blood inside was not coagulated, nor had it dried. The cube had preserved it, suspending it mid-motion like an insect trapped in amber.

"A trophy," he murmured.

Radcliffe sighed. "That's what we're thinking, too."

Tucton leaned against the doorway, arms folded. "So, what's our genius consultant got for us, then?"

Theo didn't look up from the cube in his hand. "It's not just a trophy. It's a collection."

Radcliffe frowned. "So, these murders are all connected? The same killer profile?"

Tucton gave a small snort, "and how have you deduced all that?"

Theo exhaled, irritated. "Constrictor knot. Clean. Learned, not improvised. Hook installed in advance, no splinters. Body hoisted post-mortem, no bruising, no struggle. Victim likely knew the killer or was incapacitated, possibly drugged. Circle is exactly three feet. Measured. The floor grooves have fresh sawdust, the victim didn't do woodwork, which means the killer prepped the room. The water glass is untouched but positioned like it was offered. Someone sat on the couch after he was already dead, cushion indent hasn't settled."

He set the cube down on the mantel with a click.

"This is number six, and we're still calling it random?"

Radcliffe remained still. Tucton scratched his chin.

Theo finally turned toward them. "This isn't impulse. It's structure. The killer isn't venting they are plotting, planning, securing that kill. Then," with a nod towards the cube, "savouring it."

Tucton raised a brow. "How does someone do all that and not leave evidence behind?"

Theo's eyes went back to the body, flat and unreadable. "That's what we're here to find out."

21:54 07/03/1943
12 Bridge Road, East Hounslow

Theo hung back, watching with the same silent contempt he reserved for people who shelved books out of alphabetical order.

A team of evidence, destroying delinquents crowded the room, their boots and impatience ruining the only clean data left. He watched as one of them stepped directly into the blood circle, erasing any hint of symmetry with a single careless boot print.

Another brushed against the fireplace, dislodging a fine layer of soot. The dust drifted down like dead snow, settling on surfaces that, five minutes ago, might have told a story.

He didn't bother shouting. He had. Every time. And every time, Radcliffe reminded him, in that low, worn-out tone, that he was a consultant. Not a sergeant. Not a commander. Just an observer. His voice carried no authority.

So instead, he observed. Silently. Bitterly.

Tucton stood near the doorway, stubbed out cigarette still smouldering in the ashtray he'd balanced on a stack of evidence folders. He was grinning slightly, watching Theo without saying a word.

Radcliffe, to his credit, was trying to maintain order, but supervising a festival of idiots didn't lend itself to control.

When the body was finally lowered and stretched out beside the hearth, draped loosely in a canvas shroud, and left to wait for a morgue van that was already fifteen minutes late,

Theo stepped forward.

He adjusted his gloves, crouched beside the body, and began.

Five foot ten. 30's.

Male. Brown hair, blue eyes. Pupils slightly dilated, but no burst vessels.

No petechiae. Not strangled.

He pried the jaw gently. Teeth yellowed and brown, more staining on the right side, likely cigars. He noted a faint scent of dried smoke at the collar.

Lips cracked. Tongue dry. Dehydration.

The glass of water hadn't been for the victim,

It was intended for a guest, the killer.

He felt eyes on him. Radcliffe, watching with that calm weight behind his stare. Tucton leaned in, expectant. They were waiting for something useful.

Fine.

He moved lower, lifting the victim's hands with practiced ease.

Fingernails clean.

No dirt, no skin. No struggle.

The victim never raised a hand. Or never had a chance to.

The trousers were well-fitted. Tailored. Pricey. He checked the stitching along the waist, custom work, recent. The pockets were tight, too narrow for comfort. The kind of suit you wore to be looked at, not to be useful.

He forced his hand into the left pocket.

Wallet.

Pen.

He pulled them both out carefully and set them beside the body.

The wallet held a few folded pound notes and a couple of shillings. One sixpence.

Well off. Not extravagant. No receipts, no photos. No family. Or none worth remembering.

He picked up the pen. A heavy fountain pen, black lacquer with a silver inlay. Expensive. Not flashy.

He turned it slowly in his hand until he found the engraving:

To my beloved son.

Theo stared at the inscription for a moment longer than he intended.

He looked at the wear. The tip was still sharp. No signs of regular writing. It had been carried, not used.

Kept close. Not shown.

A gift from someone important, but not someone still present.

Father? Dead? Estranged?

A symbol. One the victim couldn't quite let go of, but didn't know what to do with either.

He tucked the pen into an evidence bag without comment.

The right pocket was worse. He angled his wrist awkwardly and extracted a blue National Registration Identification card, the new kind, rolled out earlier in the year.

The card was crisp. Barely creased. Still smelled faintly of new paper and ink. Only one stamp on the back-dated 1943.

He turned it over and read aloud under his breath:

Name: Michael John Dyer

D.O.B: March 2nd, 1908

ID Number: 0145, 827, 391

Address: 12 Bridge Road, East Hounslow

Occupation: Chartered Accountant

East Hounslow. Wealthy side of the village. Bridge Road was lined with detached houses and overgrown hedgerows, not a place you rented, and certainly not where you stayed if you had a family to feed.

Chartered accountant matched the suit, the shoes, the pen, the silence. A man who made good money and spent it only where it couldn't be judged.

Theo read the card twice more, then sealed it in the bag.

Everything about Dyer said precision, order, predictability.

He said nothing, but already the web was forming.

Michael was well-dressed, recently updated his documents, alone, no defensive wounds. The killer had been expected. Or at least not feared.

Radcliffe and Tucton had started toward him, to ask if he had done their job for them, when something caught Theo's eye.

He moved without a word, weaving through the crowd of uniformed incompetents still trampling the crime scene like tourists at a market. Their laughter and loud instructions faded to a low hum as his focus narrowed.

In the entranceway, near the base of the stairwell, stood a plain set of drawers. Waist high. Six thin compartments, built more for letters and keys than storage. Five of them looked untouched, edges clean, varnish intact. But the top left drawer, closest to the front door, had worn edges. The paint was slightly chipped, the handle polished by habitual use.

Theo crouched slightly and opened it.

Inside was a scatter of everyday clutter. But clutter had

context.

At the top, folded neatly, was a receipt from the Inwood Events Hall, dated one weeks ago. An attendance confirmation for a financial management conference. The victim had listed his name and company, signed in, stayed until the closing panel. Noted.

Beneath it, an older, buff, coloured National Registration Identification card. The previous model. The same name and ID number as the blue one pulled from his pocket. Several stamps on the back, the last issued in 1942. Worn but intact.

A shallow handful of copper pennies and farthings, tarnished by time and use. Probably dropped there every evening. Routine. Small comfort. People with structured minds often had a place like this, a drawer where time accumulated.

Theo's fingers touched the edge of a folded envelope. A letter, handwritten in a formal script. The paper was creased three times and yellowing at the corners. He opened it carefully and scanned the content.

A letter from his father.

Structured prose. Formal tone. A strained warmth. The sort of letter written by a man more accustomed to ledgers than affection. Near the end, a line stood out:

"I hope this pen serves you better than I ever did."

Theo's gaze drifted toward the evidence bag holding the fountain pen.

The old man was deceased. This letter was closure, or a failed attempt at it. Based on tone and phrasing, it came posthumously. Possibly part of the will. A final gesture to patch over guilt. But the pen had never been used. Just carried. Held. Carried again.

He folded the letter back as it was.

Two wartime ration cards. The stubs were mostly spent

but kept deliberately. Not tossed, not hidden. Just filed away with everything else.

Organized, or discarded because he could afford to eat out. A man with money didn't always need to cook. He ate at clubs, business luncheons, or hotel cafes where the cards weren't always demanded. But he kept them anyway. For order. For routine.

Or maybe for appearances.

At the bottom of the drawer was a small red envelope. No stamp. No address.

A Valentine's card.

Inside, short verse. Not poetic. Just hopeful. The handwriting was small, careful, neat, but distinctly feminine. The curvature on the Gs, the way the tails of the Ys flicked upward before stopping. Uniform spacing. Left-hand slant.

Theo examined the strokes more closely. Office worker. Used to forms. Used to keeping lines even. She'd written this with effort. With care.

He paused, head tilted.

Unsent. Or returned.

Footsteps approached behind him. He didn't turn.

Tucton's voice was first. "Been busy, Theo?"

A new cigarette hung from his mouth, unlit but twitching as he spoke.

Radcliffe stood beside him, arms folded.

"We need a lead this time," the inspector said, kindly.

Theo stood, handing over the NRI card and receipt. "Michael Dyer attended a convention at Inwood Events Hall three weeks ago. Accountant. Likely frequented that space. The killer could've followed him there. Might've met him there."

He nodded toward the letter and pen, now bagged.

"The pen was from his father. Deceased. Based on the tone of the letter, their relationship was strained. The gift was posthumous, guilt motivated. Something worth investigating. Probate records might show more."

He lifted the red card slightly. "This was never sent. Or was returned. A secret admirer. The writing style suggests an office worker. Consistent, practiced, deliberate. Someone who thought about their words. Possibly someone nearby. Possibly someone who saw him as more than just another suit."

Tucton raised a brow. "So, Pen from a dead dad. Mystery woman who likes bad poetry. And a drawer full of receipts. You really know how to pick the winners."

Theo didn't bother responding. He adjusted his cuffs instead.

"I need to mull things over," he said, brushing past them. "Tucton, try not to ruin the investigation before I solve it."

Theo walked out of the building and made for his car. Pulling his coat tighter to fight the chill growing in the air.

There has to be something he missed, or more likely is being obscured. For now.

2. FAMILIAR STRANGERS

6:12 09/03/1943
17 Ellington Road, East Hounslow

"You haven't slept again, have you?"

The voice cut through the clutter of Theo's thoughts like a thread drawn tight. He didn't move. Not at first. He was seated cross, legged atop the kitchen table, eyes closed, back straight, breath shallow.

The visions weren't hallucinations. They were reconstructions, images stitched from observation and memory. The body, the rope, the blood, the desk drawer. All rotating behind his eyes like a diorama in motion. He'd been there for forty-seven minutes.

A warm weight pressed into his hands. Fingers he hadn't consciously moved closed around a ceramic mug.

"Morning, D," Theo murmured, opening his eyes.

He took a swig. The bitterness struck immediately, sharp, and acidic. He recoiled, lips curling.

"No milk?"

Darrell's voice floated back from the countertop. "We used the last of the rations for your oxidised lactose experiment, remember?"

He was cleaning something, quiet, rhythmic motion, half

ritual, half necessity. Theo turned his head toward the sound.

"However," Darrell added, "the moisturiser you made has worked a treat."

He held up his hands, inspecting them as though admiring a work of art. Skin un, cracked. No flaking. Theo gave a faint nod.

Behind him, the wall had become a makeshift incident board. No pins or red string, he found those theatrical, but pages of notes, photographs, and evidence sleeves were arranged with absolute spatial logic. The paper spacing was millimetre consistent. Grouped by location, victim age, time of death. Cross, referenced by category, not chronology.

It still wasn't enough.

He stared at the wall. Each item existed. Each fact was true. But the line, the thread that ran through all six murders, remained elusive.

He reached for it mentally. Nothing held.

"Eggs?" Darrell asked, not looking up.

"And bacon."

"Alright. I'll do toast too."

Theo's stomach rumbled. The sound irritated him. It reminded him of biology, of needs that got in the way of better work.

He shifted, turning on the table while uncrossing his legs and lowering himself flat against the table, limbs loose, the mug still in one hand. His head dangled just over the edge, spine curving slightly.

The room inverted.

From this angle, the world lost its rules.

Angles tilted. Shadows pooled differently. The grid of evidence on the wall became something else entirely, less a chart, more a constellation. Fragments of dead stars, waiting for names. Waiting for order.

He let his mind drift, not aimlessly, but with surgical detachment. Into numbers. Into statements. Into still photos of faces that no longer existed. The map he'd drawn of the murder sites. The layouts. The post-mortem reports. The interviews with people too slow to understand what had been taken from them.

It should have spoken by now. It should have screamed.

But it didn't. Not yet.

Then, a knock at the door. A dull, idiotic interruption.

"Door," Theo said, not moving, not blinking. Still staring at the web.

"I'm making your breakfast," Darrell called over the sizzle of eggs. "You live here too, y'know. You'll have to answer it."

"Busy."

The skillet cracked loudly in reply. "If my eggs aren't runny because of this, I swear to Christ, Theo, you won't see your next birthday."

He muttered the rest as he walked out. "Not that you celebrate it anyway…"

Theo sat up slowly. Feet hit the floor with a soft thud. He crossed the kitchen in silence and stood before the wall.

That was it.

That was the piece he hadn't seen.

Michael Dyer. Thirty-five.

His eyes moved across the top row of pinned cards, each marked only by first name and photograph.

Eleanor. Seventy-five.

Marian and William. Sixty-five.

Thomas. Fifty-five.

George Forty-five.

Michael. Thirty-five.

A staircase. Not symbolic. Mathematical.

Ten-year intervals. Killed alone.

Except Marian and William, killed together. The only deviation.

He stared at the names. He knew them all. Knew the dates, the locations, the method.

But he hadn't looked at the ages in sequence. Not like this. Not inverted.

This wasn't random. This was ritual. A list.

A countdown.

And if it held, if the pattern didn't break, then the next name would be twenty-five.

Then fifteen.

Then five.

Three more deaths. Three more carefully chosen lives drained and preserved in cubes like insects in amber.

A child's blood in a cube.

That's where this was going.

Theo stepped back. His jaw tightened.

He didn't believe in fear. He didn't trust it.

But the idea of finding a five-year, old child, bloodless and strung up like the others, touched something in him he couldn't catalogue or dissect.

Something old.

Something buried.

And the worst part? He could see it. He could already see it.

The rope. The angle of the neck. The perfect circle of blood on a nursery floor.

He shook it off. Hard.

Not yet.

Three more bodies before it ended, unless he ended it first.

But to do that, he needed to find the next name.

And time wasn't a luxury anymore.

"Do we know anyone who has turned or Is turning twenty-five this year?" Theo asked, turning from the wall.

The room was empty.

Darrell was gone.

The kitchen smelled like burning oil.

Theo walked toward the stove, smoke curling softly from the pan. The eggs had gone past salvageable, whites rubbery, edges charred, yolks greyed and caved in. The skillet sizzled weakly, half-hearted, like it had given up midway through the process.

He turned off the heat. Took a breath. Retrieved two plates from the cupboard.

Two slices of toast each. No crusts. Buttered evenly while still warm, enough to melt but not soak. He scooped the eggs, burnt or not, onto the plates. Laid strips of bacon on top, crisp but not brittle.

Breakfast, assembled. The ritual completed.

He had just placed the cutlery when the kitchen door creaked.

"Oooh. Breakfast."

A man with long, tangled hair and an oversized coat wandered in, plucking a strip of bacon from the nearest plate without hesitation. His hands bore ink smudges and faint bruises along the knuckles, and his boots left wet prints on the tile.

Theo didn't look at him yet. He poured two cups of tea with the precision of someone who didn't drink it.

Darrell entered next, visibly annoyed. "I told him you were working. He just pushed past me."

"It's fine, D." Theo slid a plate forward. "I accomplished something today. Eat your eggs."

Al dropped into a chair without asking. He chewed loudly. "These are good. You've gotten better. That wartime bacon used to taste like shoe leather."

Theo sat opposite, folded his hands. "What do you want, Al? Homeless again?"

Al kept chewing, spraying a fleck of bacon onto the table as he spoke. "No, not yet. But soon, probably. Apparently, people still expect to be paid on time. Can you believe that? Rude."

Darrell stabbed a fork into his eggs with force. "Let me guess. Five pounds?"

Al looked wounded. "Four. And fifteen shillings. I'm not greedy."

Darrell snorted. "Five. For more drugs, right? Are you going to pay your landlord with that?"

"I don't have a landlord. Not since he changed the locks. I still live there... technically."

Theo said nothing. He watched Al with clinical detachment. It wasn't just the mess of his coat or the smell of damp clothing. It was the ticks. The twitch in the corner of his eye. The way he licked his lips between sentences, not out of dryness, but as habit.

They had once shared benches. Blankets. Broken glass in their shoes. That was before the war, before Theo's parents had died.

Back when life was simpler. Or at least clearer.

Back when survival meant chemistry. When barbiturates came cheaper than food, and amphetamine meant staying warm without moving.

He hadn't touched any of it in years.

But Al hadn't climbed out. Not really. Just shifted the furniture around.

Theo tapped his fingers once against the table. "When's your birthday?"

Al blinked. "What?"

"Your birthday."

"Tomorrow, actually." He grinned. "You remembered?"

Theo didn't answer. He was already doing the math.

"You remembered... right?" Al's grin faltered. Just slightly.

Theo stared at him for a beat too long. Then nodded once.

"Of course," he said. "In fact, I've planned a party. Surprise. Meet me at Inwood's tomorrow. 11am."

He watched Al's face for the smallest twitch, there it was. Surprise. Caution. That was enough.

Theo stood, smoothing his coat sleeves as he turned away from the table. "I'm not eating this."

He gestured at the burnt eggs, the plate, the conversation.

"D, throw some cinnamon on it and give it to Al. The birthday boy deserves something warm before he's evicted."

Darrell opened his mouth. Al raised a hand to protest.

Theo didn't wait.

"I'll bring the five pounds tomorrow," he said as he stepped out. "Birthday present. If you turn up."

The door closed behind him before either of them could

speak.

12:00 09/03/1943
65 High Street, East Hounslow

Theo stood in the queue, hands buried in his coat pockets, shifting forward at the rhythm of steam and impatience. Hiss of milk. Rattle of ceramic. The staccato scrape of shoes against floorboards. A symphony of idle noise.

It was taking too long and so his mind drifted.

That morning, he'd visited the Inwood Events Centre. Reserved a whole day slot in one of the smaller meeting rooms, mid-afternoon, quiet, deliberately unremarkable. It had been enough to glance over the location, ready for an infiltration at another time.

A voice pulled him back.

"Hello? Can I take your order?"

Theo stepped forward, studying the girl behind the counter.

Black hair pulled into a tight bun, with wisps straying at the edges. Brown eyes with dark hollows beneath them, young, early twenties, but fatigued. There was a faint crusted stain on her collar, slightly yellowed.

Baby spit. Formula or regurgitated milk.

The faint swell of white powder near the cuff of her sleeve, dried milk dust. She worked fast, likely oversaw the opening shift and morning deliveries.

Nails clean. Manicured. Done at home.

Likely a single mother. Working. Exhausted. Still trying to feel human.

She would make a precise cup of coffee. Efficient. Controlled.

"A large, to go. With milk, please."

"That'll be sixpence."

Theo pulled a shilling from his pocket and placed it on the counter.

"Keep the rest. For your little one."

He didn't wait for her reply. Just shifted to the side and leaned against the low iron barrier dividing the takeaway queue from the small café seating area.

He had never been inside "Filtered Grounds" before. The name hadn't meant anything until now. Too clever by half. Too ironic by design.

The place was clean. Thoughtfully arranged. White tile with pale wood trim. Brass fixtures. Glass domes over pastries no one was buying.

The café itself was quiet, two older men at the far window, speaking in low murmurs. A secretary scribbling in a planner. But the takeaway queue had grown to the door. Monday, lunchtime. A river of workers flowing back to their desks, caffeine clutched like rations.

Someone leaned against the barrier beside him.

A woman. Mid-Twenties. Casual posture. Loose hair. She glanced at him briefly, then turned her attention to the workers behind the counter, watching the assembly line of cups, lids, and steam.

Theo glanced at her. Once. Then again, longer.

Hair loose, but the curling at the ends suggested it had been tied recently. Nails short and filed smooth, neither neglected nor adorned. A cream blouse, unbuttoned at the collar, but layered over a fitted shirt. No skin revealed. No ornamentation.

Denim jeans, no signs of wear. No oil, no scuffs. Not new. Not cheap. Practical.

Her mouth held the shape of a smile, but only just. The kind worn out of habit. No dimple. No tension in the cheeks. No light behind it.

Everything about her was almost.

Almost polished. Almost relaxed. Almost present.

But nothing about her settled.

His eyes lingered a second too long.

She turned. Met his gaze.

"Can I help you?" she snapped, her voice sharp enough to turn nearby heads. "Why are you staring?"

Theo blinked once.

"You don't make sense to me."

Theo's voice wasn't loud, but it cut through the ambient noise like glass scraping across wood. The quiet around them sharpened. People glanced up, then quickly away. The kind of moment that wasn't dangerous, just strange. Unpredictable.

"Everyone else has a story," he continued, eyes fixed on her. "Clear as if written for me to read. But you..." His gaze flicked to her hand. "You rub your ring finger like you used to wear one. But there's no indentation. No discolouration."

His eyes moved to her face again. "Your smile is hollow. But welcoming."

She didn't even blink. Not right away.

Then she smiled again, only this time it touched her eyes. Something flickered there. Not vulnerability. Not amusement. Something like play.

"Do you want to go somewhere quieter to have a chat?" she asked. "I'll tell you about my hollow smile."

Theo hesitated.

The room hadn't moved, but the pressure had shifted.

"...Yeah. Sure," he said, slower than usual. "I'm Theodore Nash."

He held out a hand. Not out of habit. But because something about her demanded response.

She took it without hesitation. Her grip was cool and steady. The moment their skin met, something in his chest shifted, like falling from a height he'd never climbed, or rising into air he'd never dared to breathe.

"Maggie Shaw," she said. "You can call me Mags. I prefer the shorter version of names. Easier to handle, don't you think?" Her voice curled lightly. "Theo."

He agreed, shorter names were easier. Cleaner. More revealing. A person's choice of abbreviation said more about them than they realized.

But hearing her say his…

It did something.

The hairs on his arms stood up, unbidden. A sharp, crawling awareness rolled through him. Like the moment a song slides into a chord progression you didn't know you were waiting for. The kind that grabs your spine and doesn't explain why.

It was irrational.

And uncomfortably specific.

He made a note of the reaction, for later. For analysis.

But he didn't ask her to say it again.

Not yet.

He didn't realise he hadn't given a response until she gave a small, amused laugh. Then turned and walked toward the counter. When she returned, she was holding two cups. She handed him one.

"The woman at the till told me to give you yours. Said to

thank you. Apparently, her son's getting new clothes now."

Theo glanced back.

The young barista was watching from behind the counter, trying to catch his eye. He didn't meet her gaze.

He turned and walked out the door.

Gratitude wasn't necessary. She should be content it happened at all.

It'd be a better world if people didn't do things to be thanked.

Especially if it wasn't an expectation to receive words that meant nothing to him.

He had turned away after giving her the change.

Couldn't she read the signs of a man who didn't want the attention that followed a good deed.

He pondered his true feelings about a struggling mum able to buy new clothes for her son.

Three buildings down, he realized he was being followed.

He stopped. Turned.

And nearly collided with a woman.

"Oh, sorry," she said, stepping back only slightly. "Were we not going this way?"

Theo narrowed his eyes. "You were following me."

Mags grinned, unbothered. "Of course. We agreed to go somewhere quieter, remember? I was following you to that place." She sipped her coffee. "Don't tell me you're one of those... what do they call it, chorizo? Schizo-pheonix things?"

Theo blinked.

She tilted her head, teasing. "You know... the ones who forget conversations and rise dramatically from their own confusion."

He didn't respond. Was that an intentional pun to cover her attempt at not knowing the word?

Her grin widened. "Relax. I'm joking. Probably."

They stood there a moment longer.

Theo studied her again, this time in profile. Still couldn't place her. Still no clear read.

And that, more than anything else, made him want to keep walking beside her.

As they walked, Theo's mind turned over possibilities, language patterns, posture, tonality. Every word she spoke was a brushstroke in a portrait he couldn't yet see clearly. He didn't like the uncertainty, but he was drawn to it.

"So, what's your profession?" Mags asked, sipping from her cup, eyes forward.

"Consultant," Theo replied. "For the police."

She tilted her head slightly. "Oh?"

"It's more of a hobby," he added. "I only get paid on freelance jobs. Case by case."

"That sounds interesting. So, you profile bad guys? Work crime scenes?"

Her shoulders shifted subtly, angling toward him. Full attention. Engaged. Comfortable.

"Yes," he said. "That kind of thing."

She looked ahead again, thoughtful for a moment. "Profile me."

He stopped. Not physically, but mentally. Pivoted.

"I mean," she added, "you already started with the hollow smile and missing ring. Go on. Tell me who I am."

Theo's gaze flicked to her face. Her tone was playful, but her posture didn't loosen. She wanted to be read, needed it, maybe. But she was also testing how well she could remain invisible while being seen.

He took a breath. No flourish. No smile.

"You present like someone who wants to blend in but can't help drawing attention. Your clothing is casual, but not quite right for the weather. No umbrella, despite the forecast. Jeans, clean but worn, chosen for comfort, not statement."

He continued without pause.

"You wear your hair loose, but the curls at the ends suggest it was tied until recently. You freed it just before we spoke. Possibly to appear more relaxed. Controlled spontaneity. That's contradictory."

He glanced at her hands. "No jewellery. No marks of it. But you rub your ring finger when you're thinking. That tells me you wore one often. Most likely not a wedding ring. A family token, perhaps. Or a school ring. Something heavy with meaning."

She didn't flinch.

Theo pressed on. "You engage quickly. When challenged, you escalated the confrontation, spoke loudly, forced the attention of the room. That's not confidence. That's practiced deflection. Immediately followed by the offer of a quieter place. You shifted from defence to invitation in under four seconds. That suggests you're accustomed to managing the tone of conversations."

He watched her carefully.

"You're not afraid of strangers. But you want them to think you are. That keeps you in control."

Mags blinked, then smiled. This one slower. Still soft but no longer hollow. There was shape to it now.

"Anything else?"

Theo nodded, eyes narrowing slightly.

"You're used to being underestimated."

She laughed. Not the airy kind. The kind that slips out when someone's been genuinely caught.

"That obvious?"

"No," he said. "That's the point."

"Well," she said, slowing to a stop beside a brick shop front, "I must say, that was both impressive and wildly invasive."

She was still smiling, but her tone had the faintest shimmer of challenge beneath it.

"You asked," Theo replied, matter-of-fact.

"I did..." Her voice lingered on the word, trailing off like an unfinished idea. They stopped, a pause falling between them, not awkward, just weighty. "Do you always run from uncomfortable social situations or only when someone shows gratitude?"

"I... well... it's just that I don't like the credit. I'm all for helping people but they shouldn't thank me."

"Sorry, I thought, seeing as you did me, I'd do you" She looked down and shuffled her feet a little.

"No apologies necessary, it's true. I was invasive enough, as you said, to warrant something in return."

They faced one another. Her eyes were darker than he remembered. Or perhaps the light had changed.

"Well," Theo said, stepping back half a pace. "It was nice to meet you, Mags. I've finished my drink. I'm going to go now."

Her face shifted, just slightly. A flicker of something, disappointment, maybe, but it righted itself instantly. The smile returned, lighter this time. Measured.

"Here," she said, reaching forward and catching him by the forearm.

Her fingers were warm. Not hurried, not hesitant. She

held him like someone who didn't second guess her choices.

She pulled a pen from her jeans pocket and began writing on the inside of his wrist.

"Hopefully the new automatic exchange line is working properly," she added, the corners of her mouth lifting as she wrote.

Theo stared at her.

Not because of the number. Not because of the ink.

Because his body hadn't moved. He hadn't stepped away.

She let go, capping the pen.

"Bye, Theo," she said. Then she turned, walking away without waiting for an answer.

He stood there a moment longer.

The numbers on his wrist blurred slightly in the cold.

It was impractical. Ink could smudge. Paper was better. A pencil would've sufficed. But she hadn't asked. She hadn't needed permission. She had simply written it.

It should've irritated him.

It didn't.

He looked at the digits again. Neat, balanced spacing. Written with control. No flourishes. Every number the same weight.

Calculated.

Was she always this forward?

Was he always this... still?

He filed the thought away for later.

For now, he had more pressing things to consider.

Like whether Al was going to live long enough to blow out his candles.

3. PARTY IN THE PARK

10:30 10/03/1943
Inwood Road, Inwood Park, East Hounslow

Theo arrived at the park at precisely 10:30 a.m.

Not early. Intentional.

The kind of punctuality that allowed for control without suspicion. The park mostly empty, and Darrell would already be here struggling under the weight of his good intentions.

The park itself was nothing special. Iron railings bordered a patchwork of grass, a crumbling concrete square served as a sports pitch, and half the benches were tagged with chalk or initials from people trying to outlive their own insignificance.

To the northwest, the Inwood Event Centre loomed five stories of clean brick, tall windows, and quiet secrets. The real heart of the operation. But Theo hadn't booked there. Too formal. Too expected. The room he'd secured was in a detached structure inside the park grounds: a utility hut with four walls, a roof, and barely enough room to lie convincingly.

He needed to be seen here first. Then he could slip into the main building with reason.

"Morning, D," he said as Darrell rounded the side of the hut, arms straining under a mop, a bucket, three garden hoes, and what appeared to be a set of hedge clippers tangled in wire.

"No... problem..." Darrell grunted, posture buckling.

Theo opened the hut. The answer to his unasked question

was immediate. It was a storage space, packed, disordered, neglected.

Perfect.

"This will do nicely," Theo said. "I'll have a word with them. After we're done, of course."

Darrell exhaled, visibly relieved that Theo didn't intend to just observe.

They got to work, pulling out wheelbarrows, spades, a rusted lawnmower with one blade missing, gloves that housed entire civilisations of spiders.

By the time they were done, the floor was visible. Bare concrete. Functional.

Darrell collapsed into a chair, sweat beading at his temples. "Reckon Al will come?"

"He will," Theo said. "Only because of the five pounds I promised."

He dragged a chair next to him.

"How was he after I left yesterday?"

Darrell shrugged. "Edgy. He's your friend, not mine. Left as soon as he cleared his plate."

Theo gave a short nod. "Thank you for tolerating him."

"It's good for the brain, right?" Darrell smirked. "Being uncomfortable and all."

Theo offered a thin smile in return. They had discussed the effects of uncomfortable situations causing strenuous activity within the mind last week, during another late-night problem-solving session. Darrell had been interested in Theo's theories on how to get the mind working, so he didn't mind some of the more eccentric methods utilised to get the subconscious into gear.

Darrell watched him for a second longer than necessary.

"So, Maggie. That encounter yesterday. That was another experiment to stimulate your logic pathways?"

Theo's eyes narrowed. He saw Darrell glance, almost reflexively, at the inside of his wrist, where the ink still lingered faintly.

"That was an experiment," Theo said, "but not the one you're imagining."

"There's something about her," he added. "She's wrong. Out of sequence. Too fluid to track."

Darrell grinned. "You're in love."

"God, no." Theo stood, tone clipped. "Investedly curious. She's a puzzle. I noticed everything and still missed the answer. That's what bothers me."

He moved toward the door, peering across the park toward the event centre.

"Do we have food, music, drinks?" Darrell asked, dragging chairs into a rough semicircle.

"I assumed you'd sort that. Guest list, too."

He was already plotting his next move. The excuse to enter the main building. The logs. The names.

"I'll go see what the centre can offer," Theo said. "If they fail to provide, I'll offer feedback accordingly."

Darrell looked up. There was a tightness around his eyes. Something caught between nerves and a headache. He wore the expression of a man about to be left with a wild animal and a blindfold.

Theo ignored it. Al was Darrell's problem for now.

He had evidence to gather.

The Inwood Events Centre stood like a government building that had forgotten it wasn't one. Its brick façade was clean, window frames freshly painted, and a brass plaque outside announced the week's schedule of financial planning workshops, charity auctions, and amateur dramatics.

Theo adjusted his coat, scanning the front entrance as he approached. Two doors. One locked, the other propped open for staff. The scent of old carpet and lemon disinfectant wafted out.

Inside, the lobby was quiet. A receptionist, early fifties, auburn bob, floral scarf, sat behind a curved desk, staring intently at a crossword. Behind her, pinned across the cubicle walls, were at least nine different photos of the same long, haired tabby cat, each in a different seasonal outfit.

To her left, a small laminated plaque:

Welcome Desk - Ask here for bookings, records & guest services.

Theo didn't pause. He walked past at a slow, unremarkable pace, noting the layout and any adjustments to his previous visit.

Down the hall: a janitor's trolley, unattended, parked beside a supply closet with the door ajar. Mops, gloves, uniform shirt folded over the top rail. He didn't need it yet. But noted it.

First, recon.

A narrow stairwell to his right led up to a mezzanine. He took it. Slowly. Quietly. He knew from previous recon that this position gave him a vantage into the reception office without being noticed too much.

From the overlook, he had a clear line of sight to the receptionist and the door behind her labelled:

Staff Records & Scheduling – Authorised Personnel Only

Exactly where the older logbooks would be.

He returned to the hallway. The janitor hadn't returned.

He took the shirt, gloves, and cap.

Slipped into the store closet and pulled them on without

hesitation. Looked like a poor fit, but passable. Mismatched janitor uniforms were not uncommon. Plausible deniability.

Then he returned to the lobby, pushing the trolley as if he belonged to it.

The receptionist looked up, halfway between suspicion and boredom.

"Bit of a mess near the west stairwell," he said. "Someone spilled coffee. Might stain."

She blinked, then nodded toward a hallway Theo had just come from "Mop closets down that way. You need a key?"

Theo shook his head. "Already cleaned it. Just heading to file an incident form. Won't take a second."

She smiled faintly. "Make sure to note it for Derek. He gets fussy when we don't log the mop usage."

He gave a nod, parked the cart against the wall and pushed through the door marked for staff.

That was close, he had banked on cleaning staff being rotated regularly during war time.

The room beyond was lined with filing cabinets and low shelves. A calendar was pinned to the far wall with event titles scribbled in block letters.

Theo moved quickly.

The records office was empty, for now.

He found the event logs in a filing drawer labelled Public Bookings. Thick books, week by week. Handwritten names, times, and purposes.

He started with the most recent and decided to work his way through the dates near to the victims' deaths.

Michael Dyer – Finance Summit - 01/03/1943 - Signed in: 12:46 p.m. – 7 days before death.

He flipped back.

Marian Nash – Local History Society talk – 7 days before death.

So, she was the target. William had been collateral, no that's not right, the killer had expected there to be two bodies that day. They were meticulous in their details, no alternatives to scratch their itch. He continued through the names.

Thomas – Rotary Club – Fundraiser – Signed in 7 days prior to his Death.

George – Gardening Lecture.

Eleanor – Knitting & Rations Workshop.

Every victim. Seven days. Exactly.

Theo straightened.

This was predator stalking prey.

His fingers hovered over the most recent logbook, the current week. The same pattern would mean a new victim's name might already be written.

He opened it.

And stopped.

There, signed in for today, in a hurried but unmistakable hand:

Alfie Cartwright – 10/03/1943 - Birthday Party – 11:00a.m.

Al was now bait, no family, no home, no one to miss him.

He would have to watch his friend closely and see who would speak to him.

But as he turned, a voice echoed from the hall.

"Janitor?"

Theo froze.

The receptionist.

Theo stepped into the hall, his face perfectly still.

"I think someone's cat's stuck in that tree outside," the receptionist called out from behind the desk, eyes wide with maternal urgency. "Looks just like the one in my photo! Can you check? It's making such a racket, bless him."

"Of course," he said.

There, just past the walkway, stood the tree. Lean, brittle, looking. Sure enough, a tabby cat sat perched on one of the lower branches, tail flicking in rhythm with its irritation.

It saw him.

And jumped down with sudden ease, landing soundlessly on the grass. No mewling, no noise. It slinked off along the edge of the building without a backward glance.

Theo watched it vanish.

Then turned.

Through the open doorway, he saw the receptionist once again hunched over her crossword puzzle, pen in hand, utterly absorbed. No sign she was waiting for a report.

He didn't linger, just turned and walked away, quiet, and unhurried, already slipping back into the rhythm of control.

11:13 10/03/1943
Inwood Road, Inwood Park, East Hounslow

Theo had stripped off the janitor's uniform in the alley across from the Inwood Events Centre. He rolled it neatly, gloves, cap, shirt, and slotted it through the bars of the iron railing.

Someone would find it. Someone would return it.

Everything found its way back eventually.

He crossed the park at a steady pace, heels tapping a quiet beat on the stone path. As he approached the hut, voices filtered out. Laughter, forced. Conversation with too many silences between the words.

Inside, the party was already in motion, if one could call it that.

Darrell, Tucton, Radcliffe, and Al sat awkwardly in a circle. Theo's gaze flicked to five unfamiliar faces, locals, most likely. People D had scraped together from nearby benches or businesses. None of them looked like they wanted to be there.

Theo stepped through the doorway.

D frowned at first, then let out a short laugh and moved toward the side wall. Tucton and Radcliffe stood as soon as they saw him. Al did too, grinning with wide, expectant eyes.

Theo didn't stop moving.

Al stepped up and opened his arms for a hug.

Theo recoiled immediately, raising a hand. Contact was not on the agenda.

Instead, he extended a handshake, brief, firm, formal.

"Thanks, Theo," Al beamed. "This is the best birthday ever. Have you got me a present?"

"You're welcome." Theo reached into his coat. "Here's your five pounds."

He pulled out the notes, crisp, neatly folded. "For rent?"

Al's eyes locked on the money, brightness shifting to something hungrier. His fingers closed around the bills, but Theo didn't let go.

He watched.

Watched the twitch at the edge of Al's mouth. The dilation in his pupils. The flicker of anger that cracked through his mask like heat through glass.

He expected Al to yank, maybe lash out.

But Al just sagged.

He dropped into a chair, the money sliding from his hand to the floor.

"I'm sorry," Al muttered. "I lied. It's for drugs. I've been homeless for months. I've been sleeping at..."

His eyes snapped toward Radcliffe and Tucton, both still in uniform.

"Erm... nowhere."

Theo nodded once. No emotion. Just assessment.

"It's okay, friend. You can stay at mine."

Al blinked.

"That is my birthday present to you," Theo continued. "D probably won't mind. Admitting the problem is step one. I'll look after you while you recover."

He placed a hand on Al's back.

It was rehearsed. Not for Al's sake, but for the audience.

It would be enough to earn trust. Enough to let him keep watch.

Al sniffled, trying to smile. "Thank you. That means... that means a lot."

Theo gave him a pat. One tap. No more.

"Go," he said. "Tell D the good news."

Al jumped up, face alight with what passed for happiness. Too quick. Too bright. His eyes kept darting, not to Theo, but to the money Theo still held.

Theo didn't miss it. The emotions that had passed through Al in the last sixty seconds had moved like harsh weather: fear, greed, guilt, hunger, and now optimism, a dangerous kind. Not hope. Strategy.

Al thinks this is a con. That all he has to do is play nice, act clean, and the money will keep coming.

Theo was already ahead. He'd moved his cash stash the night before. Darrell's too, after noticing the idiot kept it stuffed in the biscuit tin. He'd tell him later.

Al walked off with a bounce that was too precise, too exaggerated. A performance.

Theo had seen better actors with worse motives.

From the corner of his eye, he caught movement. Radcliffe and Tucton stepped forward from the circle, their posture all business.

"Can we chat for a moment?" Radcliffe asked. "Outside, preferably."

Theo followed.

The air was colder out here. The park quieter. Afternoon sun filtering through leafless branches like half, hearted shadows.

"Forensics came back empty," Radcliffe said, straight to the point. "Like the others."

Tucton picked up: "But the cube, resin, confirmed. Epichlorohydrin and bisphenol A."

Theo stopped walking. His mind spun for half a beat.

"Epoxy resin," he murmured. "Unusual. Unexpected."

"How so?" Tucton asked. His mouth was already tightening for a smug retort, but Theo let the silence hang. He waited, still and expressionless, until the detective's lips relaxed again.

Then he delivered the information like an autopsy report.

"Condensation of epoxides and amines was patented in 1934 by Paul Schlack, in Stuttgart. Pierre Castan furthered the research, Zurich-1936, for dental prosthetics. Functional epoxy wasn't commercially viable until '39. But bisphenol A wasn't part of the manufacturing process until 1940."

Tucton frowned.

Theo didn't slow.

"Which means access to that information would've required scientific privilege, high, level chemistry education, university research exposure, or access to journals that aren't freely shared during wartime."

Radcliffe raised an eyebrow. "So, we're looking for a German chemist? A refugee scientist?"

"No," Theo said. "We're looking for someone who reads. Extensively. Someone who didn't need to invent epoxy to understand it. Someone like me. Someone who reads chemical journals for recreation."

Tucton let out a scoff. "So basically... anyone."

Theo turned, voice flat. "Not anyone, Tucton. You, for example, only purchase magazines with women in swimsuits and titles like 'Pictorial Weekly.'"

Tucton's mouth opened, then snapped shut.

"Enough," Radcliffe said, cutting through. "Tucton, pull records. Anyone attending evening chemistry courses, or applying for lab positions, even book orders for science texts. Find out who's buying these chemicals. If they can't get them locally, someone's selling."

Tucton nodded sharply. "Sir." He turned and strode off, boots crunching across the gravel.

Radcliffe exhaled. "You didn't have to humiliate him."

"I didn't," Theo replied. "That was mercy. If I'd tried, he'd be crying."

Radcliffe laughed despite himself. "You're unbelievable."

"I prefer the term efficient."

Radcliffe shifted tone. "What have you got for me?"

Theo considered. No point in holding back now. The more people looking, the better.

"The victims were chosen by age. Nothing else. Seventy-five. Sixty-five. Fifty-five. All descending by ten years. The killer is moving backward through life, possibly symbolically. Possibly not."

Radcliffe's expression sharpened. "You're sure?"

"Yes. The next victim will be twenty-five. After that-fifteen. Then five."

Radcliffe swore under his breath.

"There's more," Theo said. "Every victim had attended an event here, at Inwood. Exactly seven days before their death. The killer either works here, has access to the guest records, or attends enough events to spot and select their targets. That's how they're keeping to the pattern."

Radcliffe's jaw tightened. "And you're telling me this now? After I've sent Tucton off chasing chemistry tutors?"

Theo met his gaze evenly. "He was going to chase something. At least now it's something productive."

Radcliffe folded his arms. "Remind me why I keep letting you do this."

Theo's expression didn't shift. "Because I get results."

Radcliffe sighed. "Alright. Let's get eyes on everyone working here. Quietly. If one of them is the killer, I want their next move to be a mistake."

Theo nodded once, already moving back toward the hut.

The countdown had started ticking again.

Six days left.

"Hang on," Radcliffe said suddenly, freezing mid-step. "Your homeless friend... he's twenty, five."

Theo didn't respond.

"No one's going to miss him," Radcliffe continued, pacing. "Is that why you invited him to your house? You're setting a trap."

Theo smiled, small, reserved. Like a father whose child just solved their first puzzle.

"You'll make a fine detective one day, sir. If we put him in custody, the killer chooses someone else. Right now, we have the upper hand. If you insist, have some officers watch the house. Quietly."

Radcliffe stared. "You orchestrated this without telling me."

"It's the logical thing to do."

Radcliffe muttered something and started pacing again, faster this time.

Theo didn't interrupt. He knew the conclusion would match his own. It would just take longer for Radcliffe to arrive.

James Radcliffe was a fine detective. With a little tuning, he could become legendary.

"Fine," Radcliffe snapped. "I don't like it. But if we're going to catch the killer, we need Al under distant supervision. Two on the front, one at the back. If it goes south, it's on you."

"If that eases your conscience," Theo said mildly, "then yes. It's on me."

"I need a sandwich. And a drink."

Theo glanced toward the hut. "D has sorted that."

The scent hit him as soon as they stepped inside. Cucumber sandwiches and warm alcohol. A bizarre pairing, one muted, one aggressive, like two personalities trying to coexist in too small a space. It lingered thickly in the air, soaking into the wallpaper, the people, the furniture. A platter of sandwiches sat to one side, sweating under a glass dome. The bread had gone soft around the edges. Bottles of beer clinked with idle movement. No ice.

Theo moved toward Darrell to ask, out of obligation, how he'd arranged it all so quickly. But the question died before reaching his lips. Darrell was shaking hands with a thin teenager in a green apron. INWOODS CONVENIENCE STORE was embroidered in darker green thread. That explained everything.

Theo slowed.

Darrell turned, saw him, and grinned with exaggerated performance. Then he pointed at Theo like a showman introducing the guest of honour.

The boy smiled politely.

Something was wrong. A thread tugged at the hem of Theo's attention. A discrepancy in the details.

Darrell held up four fingers and laughed. Four pounds. Theo reached into his coat, pulled out four notes, and handed them over without breaking stride.

He scanned the room again. Something had shifted. A detail had changed. Something, someone was where they shouldn't be.

There.

Blonde hair. A ponytail. A woman with her back turned, speaking to someone near the beer table.

His body moved before his mind did. Each step pulled him deeper into the sensation that he was late for something. That he'd missed the moment by milliseconds.

He reached her. Tapped her shoulder.

She turned.

Blood.

It poured up her face, defying gravity, thick and arterial. His mother's face. Skin waxen. Her expression vacant.

His lungs locked.

And then, blink.

Gone.

No blood. No corpse.

Just Maggie, standing there with that same gentle amusement in her eyes. No shock. No confusion. Just observation.

"Mum?" he said, voice too soft, too dry.

Her brows knit, just faintly.

"No," she said gently. "Do I look like her?"

Her voice grounded him. Not the words, the tone. Playful. Soft. Unconcerned.

Maggie.

Of course it was.

His mind ran diagnostics in silence.

Thirty-six hours, minimum.

No REM sleep.

Symptoms: micro sleeps, cognitive slips, visual hallucinations.

Uncommon for him. Rare. But not impossible.

A stress hallucination. Fragmented grief surfacing without warning. His subconscious responding to proximity, hair colour, angle of her jaw, posture under yellow light.

Logical. Measurable. Contained.

"Sorry," Theo looked into her eyes, "I don't wish to offend but why are you here?"

She smiled, unbothered. But her eyes flicked over his shoulder.

Theo turned.

Darrell.

Of course.

Drink in hand. Grinning. A nod, his hand raised as if to toast. Bastard.

"He read the number off my wrist," Theo muttered, half to himself. "Called you."

Maggie shrugged. "He's a good man. Said you deserved a gift too."

There was something practiced in her tone. A woman used to matching energies in any room. Shifting temperature as needed.

She tilted her head, studied him. "So... how have you been?"

Theo answered, but the words were automatic. "Good, thanks."

"Nice of you to come," he added.

"Darrell said Al's turning twenty-five, right?"

"Right," he echoed. Then she slipped her arm through his like it had always belonged there.

He froze for half a second. Then let her.

Her arm was warm. Her touch deliberate.

She guided him gently, as though she'd been here before.

He said nothing.

She glanced up at him. Smiled again. Softer this time.

"You know," she said, "I'd like to meet your mother sometime. She sounds lovely."

His stomach turned a quiet revolution.

He couldn't answer.

He didn't trust his voice not to crack and he didn't crack.

So, he said nothing at all.

Either ignoring the silence or understanding it, Mags escorted them out of the hut and into the park.

"Fancy a walk?"

Theo nodded and let her lead on.

4. RATIONED RATIONALE

8:25 11/03/1943
17 Ellington Road, East Hounslow

"Is he still asleep?" Darrell stumbled into the kitchen, one hand dragging through his hair, the other cradling his forehead.

"Yes," Theo said without looking up from the paper. "Like you, he had a bit to drink."

Theo had, as always, been up since 6:30. Routine did not accommodate hangovers.

He'd dressed. Eaten porridge, measured precisely, one spoon of jam stirred in clockwise. Brushed his teeth. But this morning, the sofa had been occupied, so he'd migrated to the kitchen table for his usual ritual: local stories, obituaries, the crossword.

"Do we have any aspirin? Or ergotamine?" Darrell mumbled from the stove, eyes squinting at the kettle like it had personally offended him. "I think I drank more than I remember. Where did all that booze come from?"

"Top drawer by the door," Theo replied. "Mags and I went to get more. She suggested the party needed oiling to get the gears moving. Everyone was seated in silent agony. I agreed."

A groan drifted in from the living room.

Theo didn't glance up. "Our guest has awoken. Prepare

him coffee, a glass of water, and two aspirin. Both of you need to be functioning today."

Darrell retrieved the aspirin, then gave Theo a sideways glare. "Why?"

"Observation. Civility. And because I hate the sound of groaning."

He gave a small nod, as if punctuating the statement with a period.

"I'm not babysitting your stray friend while you run off across town flirting with women," Darrell muttered, shaking two tablets into a chipped saucer.

Theo turned a page in the paper. "What about while I earn our rent?"

Before Darrell could respond, the sitting room door creaked open, revealing a shape that vaguely resembled Alfie Cartwright. Less man, more animated corpse.

Al shuffled in like a sleepwalker, hair flattened on one side, the other side of his face streaked with dried drool. His clothes were the same as yesterday, possibly the same as last week. The smell hit Theo's nose like a slap.

He recoiled, subtle but immediate.

Darrell, less restrained, scrunched his face so tightly his features nearly imploded. He slammed the drawer shut with a thud and bolted from the room, feet slapping across the floor and up the stairs in retreat.

Theo blinked after him.

"Morning, Al. Feeling alright?" he asked, voice even, turning to remove the now, whistling kettle from the stove.

Al groaned and collapsed into a chair like a dying man, head buried in his folded arms, hiding from the daylight like a creature of the crypt.

"Been worse," he muttered, breath warm and sour.

Theo moved efficiently, measured water into a chipped mug, stirred in a spoonful of instant grounds, and laid out the aspirin and a second glass of water. He placed all three in front of Al, who responded by immediately snoring into the table.

Theo frowned.

Then jabbed a precise finger into the soft space between two ribs.

Al shot upright with a yelp, eyes wide in brief alarm before scrunching in pain.

"Wha'di'ya do that for?" he whined, rubbing his side.

"You were asleep again. That wasn't the arrangement," Theo said flatly, sitting back down.

Al reached for the water and slurped it like a man dying of thirst. Half of it ran down his chin and soaked the collar of his already, suspect shirt.

"Drink. Take the aspirin. No, there isn't more. Then go bathe and put on fresh clothes. You stink."

Al wiped his mouth with the back of his hand, nodded blearily, and gasped, "Thanks, Theo."

He sounded like someone who'd been rescued from drowning, grateful but still unsure which direction was up.

Theo sipped his own tea and returned to his newspaper.

They sat in silence.

Al sipped his aspirin water like each swallow was an act of heroism. When he finally drained the glass, he stood with a grunt and shuffled out of the room, trailing the scent of stale sweat and regret. The bathroom door clicked shut behind him.

Theo exhaled slowly, already clearing the cups.

Darrell reappeared the instant Al disappeared, hand slicing through the air like he could karate the smell into submission. He moved to the pantry, pulled out a sprig of lavender from the herb shelf, then struck a match.

Theo glanced up from the paper.

Smoke curled upward as the lavender caught, the scent slow to arrive but eventually cutting through the thick residue of Al's presence. Only once the room smelled faintly floral did Theo realise just how bad it had been.

"Good thinking, D," he said, nodding. "Crack a window too."

Darrell left the lavender smouldering in a dish on the table and moved to the window. As he lifted the sash, a sharp rush of cold air carried the smoke out and swirled the remaining stink back in.

"I wish you'd run this past me first," he said. "How long is he staying?"

"A week."

"A week?" Darrell turned from the window, eyebrows high. "I don't think I can agree to that, Theo."

"Sure you can. It's important. Detrimental to life's answers."

Darrell narrowed his eyes. "So, it's part of your case? A new experiment? Exposure to chaos and uncomfortable stimuli to unlock new levels of brilliance?"

He crossed to the kitchen table and sat down like a student awaiting an absurd lesson.

Theo folded the newspaper, neat and precise, and extended it toward him.

"It's not for me. It's part of the case, yes, but not stimulation."

Darrell didn't take the paper. Just stared.

Theo raised an eyebrow. "What?"

Darrell's mouth opened, then closed. Opened again. Finally, after a beat of stunned silence:

"He's bait?"

"Yes."

The colour drained slightly from Darrell's face.

"B-but, h-how could... why would... WHAT!?" The final word erupted like a cough that had been building for hours. Theo winced more at the volume than the outrage.

"I don't understand the question," he said honestly, placing the newspaper onto the table.

Darrell stood abruptly, pacing. His hands raked through his hair, then down his face. When he finally turned back, his expression was somewhere between laughter and a panic attack.

"Of course you don't. Of course. Logically, it makes sense, to you. But you never consider the morality of your logic, do you?"

Theo didn't respond. Not right away.

He didn't reject the accusation because it wasn't wrong.

Morality was subjective. Fragile. It bent under pressure, just like people.

But logic? Logic remained intact. And in this case, the logic was sound.

Al was a known quantity. He could be observed, contained. The police had eyes on him. Theo had control.

Letting the killer choose someone else, someone unknown, unpredictable, that was the immoral choice.

"Radcliffe approved it," he said. "Three officers posted. Front and back. And I'm here watching."

Darrell scoffed. "Watching? Where's your friend now, Theo? For all you know, he's upstairs being murdered as we speak."

"No," Theo said calmly. "We have six days before that happens."

He allowed himself a flicker of a smile. "The worst he's doing now is using your soap on his more intimate areas."

Darrell groaned in revulsion and defeat.

"So, I am the babysitter."

He reached into his coat pocket and pulled out a small silver tin.

Theo watched, then spoke without turning. "If you've finally decided to smoke in front of me instead of hiding it, please do it by the window. I'll make this week up to you. Later."

Darrell didn't answer. He crossed to the living room window without another word, cigarette between his fingers.

Theo stood. Moved to the board. Studied it again.

From the outside, this might all look cold. Calculated. Cruel.

But it wasn't.

It was structured.

A necessary variable in a controlled equation.

One life, under supervision, to stop a sequence of others from ending in silence and blood.

He adjusted one of the victim photographs slightly, realigning the pin.

People call it playing God.

He called it problem-solving.

16:56 11/03/1943

17 Ellington Road, East Hounslow

Theo's neck groaned in protest as he stood and stretched, joints clicking like gears slipping back into place. He made his way to the kitchen sink and reached for a clean glass. The water was cold, refreshingly so, and the first sip sent a chill down his spine, welcome clarity.

His stomach rumbled, low and steady. He wandered over to the fridge.

Chicken. Ham. Cheese. Not enough from which to craft a proper meal.

Sausage and mash with a bit of gravy, it was simple, hearty, and familiar. But they'd need fresh sausages and butter. He moved to the drawer where the ration booklets were kept and flipped through them, searching for the relevant coupons.

He and Darrell had made a pact at the start of rationing: no hoarding. They'd only redeem what they needed, when they needed it. It made tracking easier, budgeting simpler, and, more importantly, kept them off lists.

Sausages had only recently been added to the rationed items, which meant limited availability. He extracted the necessary slips and tucked them neatly into his inner coat pocket.

In the sitting room, Al was sprawled across the sofa, eyes locked on the television like it held answers to questions he didn't know how to ask. Darrell sat in the armchair by the bookshelf, a novel in his lap. He was clearly trying to read, but his eyes didn't move. The noise from the TV was clearly cutting through his concentration.

"Afternoon," Theo said.

"Ah, the dead stirs," Al replied, eyes still on the screen.

Darrell frowned. Mildly ironic, coming from Al.

"Need something?" Darrell asked, closing the book with a hopeful snap. He leaned forward, clearly eager for a distraction.

"Just letting you both know, I'm heading to the shop," Theo said. "Fancy bangers and mash. Do you need anything?"

"Sweets," Al muttered.

Darrell rolled his eyes. "I could do with more bread. Cheese on toast has become a lunch staple."

"Unless you've hidden a ration slip somewhere," Theo said, "we're not getting bread until next week."

"Eggs, then," Darrell said. "I'll make my own with the flour we've got."

Theo nodded. "Alright. Al, behave. D, remember our discussion."

Both men grunted in vague acknowledgment.

Theo walked toward the front door. His hand had barely touched the handle when shouting echoed from the street outside.

A woman's voice. Angry. Two male voices, sharper, louder. One barked something he couldn't catch.

Then, a knock. Firm. Rhythmic. Official.

Theo opened the door to find a blonde woman being lightly restrained by one of the plainclothes officers. The other stood in the doorway, hat in hand, face tight with awkward formality.

"Sorry to bother you, sir," the officer said. "This woman approached the building. She refused to identify herself. Do you know her?"

Theo blinked once.

Then nodded. "Yes. She's a friend. Let her through."

His voice was even. Clipped. The kind of tone that made people snap to attention.

"What part of covert," he added, "did you not understand? I'll be speaking to Radcliffe about this."

The officer stiffened. "Of course, sir. Apologies."

He turned to the man still holding Maggie back. "Let her go. She's cleared."

The second man released her immediately, stepping back with practiced deference. But Theo saw the shift, the shame in the first one's eyes, the flush of embarrassment at having overstepped. And in the second, a flicker of regret. He'd backed his partner too quickly. Wanted to act, be useful, be seen.

Neither would speak of it again.

Maggie straightened her coat and walked up the path toward the door with calm elegance, as if she hadn't just been manhandled by a pair of men playing soldier. She caught Theo's eye and offered a subtle smile, more knowing than thankful.

"I told you we needed to wait for a signal," one officer muttered to the other as they retreated. "He said if we jumped the gun..."

"Shut up," the other whispered back.

Theo stepped aside to let Maggie in. "Are you alright?"

"Oh, I'm fine," she said, brushing a lock of hair behind her ear. "Though I'll admit, I'm a little disappointed they didn't use handcuffs."

Theo blinked.

"...Did you want to be restrained?"

She laughed, light and mischievous, and gave him a playful slap on the chest. "Not yet. We haven't even kissed."

His brain stalled. Absolutely blank.

He had no mental preparation for this level of directness. No rebuttal. No clever comeback. His mind, normally an efficient engine of deduction, seized up like a gear jammed mid-turn.

Her hand lingered for a second longer than it needed to, and something moved in his chest. Not a flutter. Not a jolt.

A pulse.

Like his heartbeat had tripped, skipping forward in time.

Maggie's smile faded a touch. Her hand slipped away.

"...Are you okay?" she asked softly. "I was only messing. You looked..."

"I-I..." he stammered. His tongue felt like it had divorced the rest of him. "I haven't... what am I even saying?"

He stared down at her. Still trying to reboot.

Theo Nash. Consultant. Professional. Forensic savant. Speechless.

She eyed him carefully.

She didn't push.

She waited.

Her eyes sparkled with amusement and something else, expectation, but her stance was cautious, almost braced. Like prey ready to bolt at the first sign of danger.

Contradiction again. Always contradiction.

Her gaze said yes, but her posture was poised for no.

"I think," she said softly, "after our very long walk and talk in the park, I'd like something more."

She smiled, but it didn't soften the seriousness of her words.

"I've never done this before. Not like this. But logically, it makes sense... to be with someone you're curious about."

Theo's thoughts stumbled.

Curiosity. Logic. Yes. Those were familiar territories. Those he understood.

"Shall we start with something small?" she offered, her voice just above a whisper.

Her shoulders relaxed. Her posture loosened. She stepped forward, just a few inches, but it felt seismic.

She licked her lips, almost unconsciously. The movement hypnotised him.

His heart began to hammer.

He could feel it pounding in his chest, in his ears, in his throat.

His instincts screamed at him to flee, not because of danger, but because of exposure. He wasn't used to this. Vulnerability was messier than blood at a crime scene.

His brain fought to make sense of it. A war between biology and logic.

Was this attraction? Hormonal impulse? Desire for connection?

The sudden, irrational urge to harm the officer who had touched her flared in him, violent and primal. He hadn't expected it. Hadn't wanted it. But it was there, clawing at the edges of his restraint. He recognised it from studies, primitive male impulse to protect a mate. Evolutionary hangover.

It disgusted him. And it thrilled him.

He stared into her eyes.

"Yes," he said at last, the word absolute. Clean. Settled.

He had made a decision. One born from curiosity, yes, but also something else. Something heavier.

He wanted to understand this flutter in his chest. The twist in his stomach. He wanted to know what it meant to feel this way.

Maggie stepped into the remaining space between them.

One arm wrapped around his waist, gentle and sure. The other rose to his face, fingers tracing the line of his jaw before resting softly against his cheek.

He didn't flinch.

Didn't overthink.

He leaned in.

And they kissed.

It was not long.

It didn't need to be.

It was quiet. It was simple. And in that moment, everything Theo didn't know how to say and everything Maggie didn't need to explain was spoken in the silence between their lips.

When they pulled apart, her hand lingered. He felt breathless. Not from lack of air, but from too much awareness.

"Well," came Al's voice from the hallway, cutting through like a blunt instrument, "I did ask for something sweet."

Maggie stifled a laugh and pulled back just slightly. Theo looked at her, really looked, and found her smiling.

He smiled too. He didn't even realise he'd done it until it was already on his face.

Then he turned to Al, voice dry. "I'm going out now. Back to your usual programming. This one's finished."

He held out his arm to Maggie.

"Shall we?"

She hooked her arm in his with a grin.

As they walked down the path, toward the shop, Theo's thoughts didn't race. For once, his mind wasn't filled with calculations or timelines or crime scene reconstructions.

For the first time in his life, nothing else held his focus so completely.

5. SHADOW WORK

8:45 12/03/1943
Inwood Road, Inwood Park, East Hounslow

Theo entered the Inwood Park Event Centre with the air of a man who belonged. He wore his confidence like a tailored jacket, but beneath that was the real disguise, a clipboard, a borrowed badge clipped to his coat, and an air of official disinterest. Today, he was not Theodore Nash, freelance police consultant. Today, he was Inspector Harold Blythe from the Health and Safety Committee.

The receptionist barely looked up. That helped.

He glanced around, classic deco lobby, a little too polished. The receptionist was a woman in her early fifties, auburn hair settling around her jaw line, glasses smudged at the edge. Her desk was obsessively neat. A small, framed photo of a cat sat beside the telephone, eight others scattered around the room.

"Afternoon," he said smoothly. "Harold Blythe here to conduct a surprise review, Health and Safety, also HR want a staff welfare report. I won't be long, just need a list of operational contacts, access points, and emergency protocol documentation."

She blinked, pen still mid, air. "We weren't told about any inspection."

"That's the point of a surprise, isn't it?" Theo gave her the kind of tight smile that said, don't make this harder than it needs to be.

She hesitated, but the badge on his coat, convincing enough under pressure, won out. "Right. I'll let the staff know."

"No need to panic the whole team. Just the names of who's on today, and anyone responsible for operations. I'll manage it from there. Quiet observation gives the clearest results."

As she pulled out a typed rota, Theo made mental notes.

Receptionist: Emma Tottle.

Real Janitor: George mout.

Event Assistants: three in total. Names: Leanne Sweath, Doug Lowd, and Sonya Sheringham.

Event Planner: Maria Hartle.

Owner: Derek Renshaw.

He had his list, and immediately crossed off Emma, the receptionist.

Too many contradictions in her posture, none of them suspicious. Her right arm was set awkwardly against her side, like it harboured an old injury or a congenital stiffness she'd learned to ignore. An ailment like that left traces, in movement, in pain management, in the lines of a face. Theo clocked them all.

Add to that her collection of cat photos and lack of discretion, Emma wasn't the type who could murder someone and keep it to herself.

"Why am I being crossed off already?" she asked, watching him draw a line through her name. Her frown was genuine, a little affronted.

"Because I'm speaking to you right now," he said smoothly. "And asking you questions is half the job."

She relaxed slightly but stayed wary. "Well, if you're asking, a man came in a few days ago. Walked halfway up the stairs, like he'd forgotten something, and left again."

She pointed to the curved stairwell, the same balcony Theo had prowled from not long ago.

"And there was another one. Said he was with the police. Started asking about specific dates and events. Got annoyed when I wouldn't hand anything over without a badge."

Theo's mouth twitched. Tucton. The storm-off sealed it.

He pictured Radcliffe calmly delivering the news of Theo's progress while Tucton tried not to explode. That alone was nearly worth the whole undercover routine.

"How do they treat you here?" he asked, sliding back into the inspector role. "Good work environment? Union representation?"

She launched into a predictable speech: mild grievances, overtime complaints, no tea breaks on Saturdays. Theo took mental note of none of it.

Eventually, he straightened his shoulders, like a man wrapping up official business. "If there's anything else you'd like to add to my report, don't hesitate to call Head Office."

He took the stack of copied documents she'd printed off, emergency exits, shift rotas, staff access logs, and turned away, already disengaging.

Theo rifled through the paperwork, then stashed them neatly in his satchel.

"Thanks, Emma."

He didn't wait for a reply. He walked off briskly, clipboard tight to his side, eyes already scanning for the next mark.

He didn't have to go far.

The next name on his list, George Mout, had left a janitor's trolley outside the men's toilets. Theo slipped in, already adjusting his tone to something casual.

Inside, a man in his late sixties was bent over with a mop,

slowly working the tiled floor in practiced arcs. He moved with the care of someone used to back pain and still too proud to admit it.

"Oh, sorry," Theo said, already retreating. "Didn't mean to interrupt. It can wait."

He was halfway back into the hallway before the thought finished forming.

Too old. That much mopping took dedication, not dexterity. Whatever rig the killer used to string up their victims like showpieces would require pulley systems, upper-body strength, and the kind of balance George Mout had likely retired twenty years ago. Unless the man was hiding the physique of a mountaineer beneath his boiler suit, which Theo doubted, he could strike another name off the list.

Back in the corridor, Theo continued his slow hunt. The Centre's layout snaked like a bureaucrat's mind: corridors for corridors' sake, doors that opened to closets, locked supply rooms, a maze of laminate and echoes.

It wasn't until he reached Event Room 3, tucked near the back of the building, that he heard raised voices and the low shuffle of chairs.

He cracked the door, peeked in, then stepped inside with the grace of someone who had every right to be there.

A woman in a wheelchair was issuing crisp instructions to three young adults wrestling with table placements. Their hands were full of cutlery and confusion.

"Hello. Maria, Doug, Sonya, and Leanne?"

They turned as one, startled, then sheepish.

"I'm Harold Blythe. Head office. Surprise inspection." He flashed the badge again with the efficiency of someone used to people not looking too closely. "Health and Safety review, plus a quick check on employee welfare. Any concerns you'd like raised will be kept anonymous."

There was a pause. The three event assistants turned to Maria like children awaiting a parent's permission.

Theo watched the dynamic play out in a heartbeat.

They default to authority. Dependents, not initiators. Not one of them had the posture of someone hiding something as ugly as a body count.

He'd already mentally crossed off four more names, but the performance had to continue.

He offered a few generic follow-up questions, fire escape clarity, trip hazards, workload balance, just enough to maintain cover.

"Any unusual activity lately? People lingering where they shouldn't?"

Doug shifted uncomfortably. Leanne's eyes darted to Sonya, who was already rolling hers.

"Well," Sonya said, "someone's been stealing stationery."

"Again," added Doug.

"Probably Doug," Leanne muttered.

"No, definitely Leanne," he shot back.

Maria rubbed the bridge of her nose.

Theo resisted the urge to sigh. "Well," he said, scribbling something meaningless onto his clipboard, "I'll pass that on. Pencils and post-it notes can be dangerous in the wrong hands."

Maria gave a dry chuckle. He liked her already.

Still, none of them fit. Not the build, not the motive, not the mental makeup.

He thanked them for their time and backed out of the room, already preparing for the next face on the list.

Time to deal with the owner.

Theo slipped out of the event room and paused in the hallway, running a quick assessment of his options. The owner was next, but the health and safety act wasn't going to cut it. Someone like Derek Renshaw would either check the paperwork or make a call. Either way, the ruse would fold faster than a bad poker hand.

He needed a new angle. Not too close to his last disguise. Emma might still be behind the desk, and he couldn't risk recognition.

He opted for something more obscure.

Ian Oster the Maintenance Guy.

Theo pulled a small fake moustache from his pocket, cheap but passable, and a pot of boot polish from his satchel. Smearing it across his cheeks and jawline, he added just enough grime to make himself forgettable. Maintenance men weren't meant to stand out. He just needed the uniform.

In the next corridor, he found exactly what he needed: a supply closet holding uniforms for all trades. Janitor. Plumber. Security. Maintenance engineer.

Perfect.

He stripped off his coat and satchel, hung them carefully inside, and pulled on the heavy grey overalls. A patch on the chest read "M.ENG - INWOOD OPS." Close enough.

A minute later, he was climbing the back staircase toward the top floor, where Derek Renshaw's office overlooked Inwood Park. It was normal for the residents around Inwood, to see Renshaw stood looking out of his window, arguing down the phone at some poor soul.

At the final landing, footsteps echoed.

Theo slowed.

A man rounded the corner, bald, sharp, shouldered, lips cracked and raw. Stress had gnawed at him for years. His fingernails looked like he chewed them more than he signed paycheques.

"Hello, sir. Derek, right?" Theo lifted a hand like a traffic warden halting a vehicle.

The man stopped, brow furrowed. "Yes. What do you want? ...Erm?"

"Ian Oster," Theo said, voice thick with blue-collar grunt. "Got told there's a leak, top floor. You know anything about that?"

Derek resumed walking. Slower now, suspicious.

"Nope. Ask Emma. I don't deal with the day-to-day. I'm dealing with a surprise inspection right now, and I don't have time for, whatever this is." He brushed past.

Theo offered a nod, neutral. Let him walk. The man hadn't noticed anything unusual.

But something else had crystallised.

None of the permanent staff fit. Not physically. Not psychologically. The assistants were followers. The janitor too old. The receptionist too preoccupied. The planner bound to a wheelchair. The owner was too far removed, he didn't even know what went on beneath his own roof.

The killer wasn't a regular.

He needed names. All of them.

Caterers. Volunteers. Temp hires.

And there was only one place to find that list.

Theo made his way back down, stopping just long enough to reclaim his coat and bag from the utility closet. He slung it over one arm, the heavy overalls still hiding his silhouette.

As he approached reception, he saw Derek again, this time in a terse argument with Emma. Something about protocols. Inspection rules. The usual bureaucracy.

They stormed off together toward the event rooms, mid-sentence.

Theo didn't hesitate.

He slid behind the desk, opened the middle drawer, and found it: a thick logbook, frayed at the edges, worn with use.

The names of everyone who'd signed in and out over the past month.

He tucked it into the folds of his coat and walked out without looking back.

No alarms. No shouting. Just quiet success.

Back into the frigid air, and away.

11:03 12/03/1943
17 Ellington Road, East Hounslow

Theo stepped through the front door, shrugged off the chill of the afternoon, and moved straight to the kitchen.

He laid the logbook on the table with a sense of finality, adjusting the chair just enough so he'd sit facing his evidence wall. From here, every note, every pinned photograph, or scribbled theory could sit in his periphery, like a silent jury watching his next move.

He reached for his pens and notepad, the ritual familiar, grounding.

A long night awaited.

But something pulled his focus.

The living room door, just slightly ajar.

Through the narrow gap, he caught a glimpse of Maggie. She was laughing, her head tilted back slightly, that rare and genuine kind of laugh that carried no weight. Her gaze shifted between two unseen figures. Theo could imagine them: Al, slouched on the sofa, probably making some absurd remark, and D, stiff-backed in his favourite armchair, either confused by the joke or pretending not to find it funny.

Then came the voices.

Al's unmistakable baritone, dry and amused.

Darrell's indignant rebuttal.

Maggie again, softer now, teasing.

Theo hesitated, his hand resting on the edge of the kitchen chair.

It would be easy to ignore it. To sit back down, let the world blur into notes and ink. But something about the sound of them, their normality, their comfort, pulled at him.

He stepped forward, quietly, and pushed the door open.

Three faces turned to look at him at once.

Al's grin froze mid-sentence. Darrell raised an eyebrow, a chip halfway to his mouth. Maggie met Theo's gaze directly, her smile slow to fade, as if his arrival had been the final punchline of whatever joke she'd just told.

And for the briefest second, Theo was out of step with himself.

Not the profiler. Not the chess player with bodies for pawns.

Just the man standing in the doorway, wondering when his house had become warm enough to hold this kind of life.

"Here's the old boy now!" Darrell called out as Theo stepped into the room. "Hey Theo, look who came to see you this morning." He leaned forward and waved theatrically in Maggie's direction, grinning like he'd just presented a birthday cake with the wrong number of candles.

"I hope that's okay?" Maggie said, softening as she looked at him. Her gaze, always steady, always searching, met his like a net cast out on still waters. Somehow, it always landed.

Theo nodded, brushing a hand down the front of his shirt like there was something to fix. "Yeah, sorry I wasn't in. I was at the Inwood Event Centre, working a case."

From the corner of his eye, he caught Al giving him a look. Not quite guilt. Not quite warning. Just enough to tell him something had been said, something more than idle chit-chat.

"D and Al were just telling me how you all met," Maggie added with a small smile, nodding toward the other two men, who were now both finding something deeply interesting in the carpet.

Theo stepped further in and pulled the old footstool over by the window, choosing his seat with care, the angle was strategic. It let him face the room but not feel like he was taking centre stage.

"I suppose some of it wasn't exactly what you expected?" he asked, voice even.

Maggie giggled, a playful sound that didn't quite match her usual composure. But then again, unpredictability was part of her charm. "No, I didn't expect you to have met Al in a social house, helping him recover from his addictions only for him to relapse repeatedly. Then Darrell said you were looking for a roommate and, during one of your cases, you saw he was getting kicked out by a woman who was cheating on him. It was sweet of you to offer him free lodgings."

Theo blinked.

Not because it was surprising, but because it was carefully curated. Just enough truth to keep it honest, just enough shine to burnish the edges. A cleaner story. A better story.

He narrowed his eyes at his two friends.

Neither met his gaze. The poker faces were good, but they weren't great. The kind of awkward stillness you only get from men who know they've been caught fluffing a résumé on your behalf.

What they hadn't told Maggie was that Theo himself had once been in a worse state than Al. That he too had walked through those same doors and seen rock bottom smiling back at him. That it was Darrell, not Theo, who had opened his door and offered shelter when the weight of his past had nearly caved him in despite his wife recently cheating on him.

And yet, somehow, Theo had become the saviour in this version.

He didn't correct it.

"Shall we go upstairs?" he said, cutting the tension like he was stepping past it.

Maggie raised a brow. "You're taking me to your bedroom?" she asked with a mock gasp, her hand covering her mouth in exaggerated scandal.

Without responding, Theo took her hand and gently led her toward the hallway.

"Have fun," Al called after them with a grin so wide it could've been seen from orbit.

"Keep the doors open. I can come up anytime," D added, deadpan, before both men burst into laughter like they were back in secondary school.

Theo didn't turn around.

But the faintest, rarest smile crept across his lips.

Theo couldn't help but smile as he walked ahead, her fingers lightly brushing his as they climbed the stairs. It was subtle, but deliberate, like a wire drawn taut between them.

At the top of the landing, he opened the bedroom door and stepped aside.

She entered like someone stepping into Versailles, letting out a dramatic gasp and spinning in place to take it all in.

"Wow," she said. "Stunning. A little grey tomb of aesthetic

restraint. I'd add some daisies on the windowsill. Maybe a splash of colour, or, I don't know, joy?"

Her eyes twinkled as she turned on the spot and grabbed Theo's shirtfront, pulling him gently toward her.

He stood awkwardly as she slid her hands around his waist.

"So," he said, trying not to sound too mechanical. "What made you come round this morning? You said yesterday you'd be busy."

She raised her brows, mock-offended. "Can't a girl see her guy on a whim?"

"Yes… I suppose she could. If she wanted to."

Her answer was a kiss, or almost. She leaned in, then shifted her weight and pushed him gently onto the bed instead. The movement startled him, but not enough to protest. Her skirt billowed as she knelt on the mattress beside him.

It was warm today. The kind of summer warmth that coaxed lighter fabrics and playful intentions. The white collar of her dress framed her perfectly, and she began to unfasten it with a slow precision that wasn't quite teasing, but close.

Theo's breath caught.

Her fingers worked the buttons, one by one, drawing the fabric down over her shoulders. The skin beneath was soft, pale, and real. He stared, caught between hunger and hesitation.

He wanted this. Craved it. It wasn't new. It was a feeling he'd known before, one that had consumed him once, ruined him in pieces, and left him clawing back to a version of himself he could live with.

And that… that was what scared him now.

Suddenly, he stood.

Fast.

Too fast.

The bed creaked in protest. Maggie jolted at the movement, recoiling instinctively. For a fraction of a second, her expression warped, eyes wide, too wide, lips curling just a little too sharp. Something primal flickered through her features. Not fear.

Control, lost then regained.

And then it was gone, like a light switched off.

She smiled again. Innocent. Lovely. Almost... shy.

Theo stood by the door, his breathing even but shallow. His hand hovered near the handle.

"Are you okay? Sorry for being so forward." Maggie's voice softened as she played with the hem of her skirt, eyes cast downward, not ashamed, but cautious now. Testing the water with her toes instead of diving in.

"Yes, erm... I'm just not..." Theo's gaze wandered, settling on a faint stain on the wall. "I don't... I haven't felt like that in a long time."

She looked up, a smirk forming at the corner of her mouth. "You mean you already finished? That was quick." She winked. "Don't worry. Like you said, it's been a while."

He turned sharply toward her, catching her reaching out. Her arm dropped awkwardly when it missed his shoulder.

"No. Not that feeling," he said quickly, cheeks flushed with a mix of embarrassment and something deeper. "I haven't... done that. I meant the craving. I wanted you so badly it scared me."

Maggie's eyes flicked up to meet his, curiosity stirring behind them.

"You see..." he continued, forcing his voice to stay steady, "I was a drug addict. With Al. We... spiralled together. I've been clean for a while now. And I haven't felt that pull, that need, until you started taking off your dress."

Her brows lifted slightly, unreadable.

"So, I'm a drug to you?" she asked, tone straddling the line between flirtation and genuine uncertainty.

"No." He stepped closer, letting his hand hover near hers without touching. "You're not the drug. But you're addictive. That feeling, what you make me feel, it hit me all at once. It just... triggered something. Not a bad thing. Just sudden. And strong."

He let the words hang, afraid of what they sounded like. Afraid of what they meant.

Maggie took a moment. Then, smiling, she gave a little hop forward and landed light on her toes, both palms coming to rest gently on Theo's chest.

"Maybe we try again another time?" he offered.

"I'd like that," she said softly.

He nodded toward the door. "Come on, I'll show you what I'm working on."

She nodded back, the same smile lingering. As she followed him out of the room, she casually re-buttoned her dress,

They re-entered the kitchen, the muted sound of the television still humming from the living room.

Al and D hadn't moved.

"I can't show you everything," Theo said, pulling out a chair. "But... I'm investigating a serial killer. Six confirmed murders. A seventh likely."

Maggie's smile slipped. "That's awful. How... how do they, you know... kill them?"

There was a slight tremble in her voice. Theo clocked it.

"We believe they're drugged first. Then suspended, lifted into the air with a pulley system. Their throats are slit cleanly. Engineered with precision."

She flinched, just slightly. He kept going.

"The killer then extracts a portion of blood and suspends it in a cube. That's where the name came from, 'The Vampire Killer', the hanging upside down, draining blood. Just like a Vampire."

There was a beat. Then:

"How is the blood's dispersion prevented inside the epoxy resin as it sets?"

Theo paused.

Slowly, he turned to face her. His voice cooled.

"I didn't mention the cube was made from epoxy resin yet."

She hesitated. Then pointed hastily toward the wall of notes behind him. "I, I saw it on the board."

His eyes didn't move.

Neither did hers.

And then, she screamed.

"YOU REJECT MY BODY UPSTAIRS BECAUSE YOU WANT ME TOO MUCH, AND NOW YOU'RE QUESTIONING MY ABILITY TO READ OFF YOUR STUPID BOARD?"

Theo blinked. Her face twisted, not into sadness, but indignation. Fury, almost. But beneath that, something else. Wounded pride? Shame?

She spun on her heel and stormed for the kitchen door, pausing just before exiting.

"You can't explain everything with trauma, Theo. Sometimes, it's just you being an arse."

She was gone before he could form a reply.

The front door slammed. Hard.

A dull ache began to bloom behind Theo's eyes.

Footsteps.

D and Al emerged slowly from the living room.

D gave a single, sympathetic pat on the back. The kind that said: I'm here. But I'm not getting involved.

Al took a beat longer. Then:

"How could you take a woman like that to your bedroom and not sleep with her?"

D shot him a glare.

Theo cracked a faint, tired smile. "I blame you, really."

He moved to the medicine drawer, pulled out a box of pills. Popped two and downed them dry.

The silence that followed was merciful.

6. DISTRACTION BY MURDER

10:50 13/03/1943
42 Gresham Road, Osterley

By the time Theo arrived, the small flat was already filling with cigarette smoke and the quiet shuffle of boots trying not to disturb anything. Constables stood aside as he stepped through the threshold.

Two bodies. One flat. One hell of a mess.

Blood was soaked into the thin carpet like black oil. A broken bottle, a scorched iron, two shattered mugs, anything not nailed down had been a weapon. The woman lay crumpled near a threadbare armchair, face swollen, hair matted. The man was collapsed by the stove, shirt torn, chest and gut punctured in a dozen places.

Radcliffe was talking to two other officers, Tucton was not present. Must be working the other case.

Radcliffe moved over towards Theo,

"Hello, thought you'd like the distraction from your current case. We have our thoughts, I've always appreciated you proving us wrong, so do your thing please."

Theo didn't speak at first. He knelt beside the woman.

Her knuckles were bruised and split, skin raw. Defensive wounds mostly but also signs of retaliation. A puncher's stance.

He moved to the man. Torn shirt. Defensive wounds as well. But fewer. And his jaw, shattered, broken from a rising angle. Someone had hit upwards into the bone with surprising force.

"Another lovers' quarrel gone wrong?" a constable muttered. "Neighbours say they screamed all night. She was always accusing him of stealing her ration slips, selling off things for bottles. Poor girl."

Theo said nothing. Not yet. He rose and moved through the kitchenette. Nothing unusual, just a scorched kettle and a rusted hot plate. But on the countertop were the outlines in dust of small glass bottles, gone now. Taken. Laudanum, perhaps. Maybe even morphine, Theo thought.

His hand hovered over a teacup, overturned and half-full of coagulating blood. That wasn't from a fight. That was after.

Radcliffe entered behind him, glancing at the bodies.

"Bloody mess. They tore each other apart, by the look of it."

"Or someone finished the job for them," Theo murmured.

"Think it's one of your... cubes?" Radcliffe didn't sound hopeful.

Theo shook his head. "No cubes. No ritual. No theatre. This is real chaos."

A knock at the door announced the clean-up crew. Two young men entered with body bags, quiet, professional. They began their grim work, laying sheets down and prepping the bodies for transport.

That's when it happened.

The woman was lifted first, laid carefully onto the stretcher. Then came the man, his frame more obvious now, limp, and slight in the shoulders. His body, stripped of anger and movement, looked delicate beside hers.

Theo's eyes narrowed.

"You see it?" he asked quietly.

Radcliffe followed his gaze.

The woman was taller. Broader. Her limbs were thick with muscle and sinew. Her attacker had to punch up, likely with less weight behind each blow. The man was short. Slender. His fingers, now visible, were ink-stained. Typist? Musician?

The bruises on her, sharp, precise, didn't match his frame. And the injuries on him? Brutal, driven, unrelenting.

"She was hit by someone like her. He was hit by someone like him." Theo's voice was low. Not in awe. In certainty.

"A third person?" Radcliffe asked.

Theo nodded. "Someone smaller and slender beat him. A woman beat her. Just... possibly the same person. A small female matches the height, bruise patterns and angle of impacts on body bodies."

He watched the stretcher bearers zip the bags shut.

"Whoever did it watched them argue. Let them fight. Then finished it to look like rage ran out of control."

"And the motive?"

Theo looked back at the empty shelf and missing bottles.

"Desperation. Addiction. Or maybe someone thought they were doing the world a favour."

Radcliffe muttered something under his breath.

"Still unrelated, though?"

"Yes," Theo replied, and meant it.

This wasn't art. This wasn't a message. This was just murder.

And for once, that was all.

The front door of the flat opened again, but this time the footfalls weren't careful. They stomped. Hard. Purposeful.

Theo didn't look up. He already knew who it was.

Wallace Tucton entered the flat like he owned it, trench coat still buttoned tight despite the heat. His hat stayed on. His scowl was so sharp it might've sliced through the crime scene tape outside if they'd bothered to put any up.

"You could've waited," Tucton said, voice gravel and pride.

Theo kept his gaze on the zipped-up body bags. "You would've just gotten in the way."

Radcliffe groaned softly in the corner. He hated when they started up like this. "We're all on the same side, boys."

"Some of us more than others," Tucton muttered.

Theo straightened. "Didn't expect to see you here. I figured you'd still be wrestling for a warrant."

"I was. I was rebuffed for the warrant, and I cannot gain access unofficially. Blood policies."

Theo raised a brow. "You tried again?"

Tucton glared. "Yeah. Thought maybe a different uniform might get me in this time. Receptionist wasn't having it. Said some 'health inspector' had already been through the staff like a dose of salts. I wonder who that could've been."

Theo smirked, barely.

"Find anything?" Tucton asked, tone biting.

"No suspects among the staff. Owner's clueless, staff too junior, janitor couldn't lift a chair, let alone a body. But..." he paused, ", Emma, the receptionist, mentioned temps, caterers, and volunteers. People who sign in, use the space, but aren't part of the normal roster."

"You saw the logbook, didn't you?"

"I did more than see it." Theo patted the satchel by his side. "I have it."

Tucton's hands curled into fists, knuckles pale. "You stole evidence."

"I borrowed inevitability."

"Christ, Theo. You're reckless."

"I'm effective."

"I should arrest you, for theft."

"I should have you arrested for incompetence."

Tucton looked like he was about to bark something back, but Radcliffe stepped between them.

"This case isn't going to crack if we're measuring our egos. Let's just regroup. Where are we now?"

Theo dropped the argument, his voice unchanged. Quiet, Focused.

"No suspects inside Inwood. No confirmed outsider signatures. But the killer knows the layout. The logging files, specific booking information. The hidden names and ages. That kind of familiarity doesn't come from a casual visitor. It comes from repetition."

Radcliffe rubbed the back of his neck. "Which brings us back to your list."

Theo nodded. "Temps. Volunteers. Recurring but not permanent. People with partial access and no long-term ties."

Tucton sighed and shoved his hands in his coat. "Then we wait on a proper warrant and check the logs legally. Unless, of course, our inspector friend wants to share."

Theo handed the satchel over without ceremony.

"I'm not here to hoard. Just here to solve."

Tucton took it but didn't say thanks.

Silence stretched.

Eventually, Theo said, "I think the killers trail has gone cold now, they have entered hunter mode. A predator hiding in the grass, finding a way into their preys' life before they pounce."

Radcliffe's mouth tightened. "And you think they'll strike again?"

"They're not finished. This kind of theatre doesn't stop until the fat lady sings, or in this case a 5-year-old stops singing. I don't like that analogy. I think it will end with a child being strung up too. We need to stop this before the curtain call."

Tucton finally cracked a grim smile. "Poetic, Nash. You ever think about putting this much effort into being a nice person Instead of an insufferable arse?"

Theo didn't answer.

That was the second time someone had called him and arse, and the last thing he wanted to think about right now was Maggie.

Not the resin cube. Not her laugh at the kitchen table. Not the heat of her skin or the sharp turn of her anger. Not the strange, stupid pang in his chest when she stormed out. Not the fact that for a moment, just one, he thought she might have been the answer to something bigger than the case.

He swallowed and turned away.

"I'll see myself out," he said, voice low.

Radcliffe watched him go, then looked at Tucton. "You really know how to bring people together."

13:12 13/03/1943
17 Ellington Road , East Hounslow

Theo unlocked the front door and was immediately struck by a wave of scent, herbs, seared meat, and something floral that reminded him vaguely of summer weddings. It wrapped around him as if the house itself had exhaled.

He slipped off his coat and satchel, hung them on the nearest peg, and nudged the door shut behind him with a kick of his heel.

In the kitchen, Darrell and Al stood mid-discussion. D hovered over the stove like a chemist on the verge of discovery, while Al was carefully laying out cutlery with all the precision of a waiter who didn't trust anyone else to do the job properly.

D turned slightly at the sound of Theo's arrival. "Ah, Theo. How was the murder?" he asked, as casually as one might ask about the weather. He gave the pot a stir, then frowned and returned to it with renewed focus. "Was it connected to the other case?"

Al gave a slight nod in greeting but didn't pause his work.

Theo pulled out a chair and sank into it, glancing at the neatly folded handcloth laid out in front of him. He picked it up, used it to clean his hands, and answered, "A lovers' quarrel, but the only thing they loved more than each other was the next high. They tore each other apart for it."

D didn't look up. "Charming."

Theo waved vaguely toward the stove. "So, what's all this? I thought ration day was Monday. And unless my brain's lost all sense of time, today's still Sunday."

"Mrs. Felts bumped us up a day," D said, lifting a spoon to taste from the pot. He paused, considered, then added a pinch of salt. "Said it was the least she could do after you found her cat last month. Her words, not mine."

Theo sighed, but his tone was easy. "We agreed not to pull favours from the elderly. Still, what's done is done. Smells good. What are we having, Chef?"

"Stew," D replied. "With a bit of flair."

"I don't trust anything you describe with flair," Theo said, but he smiled all the same. "Still, I'm starving. Let's see if it kills me."

Al stood there, looking sheepish. His eyes darted to D, who returned a small nod and the kind of smile that said, you'll be fine. Al then stepped forward and laid a fourth-place setting at the table, right beside Theo's.

Theo didn't need to ask, but did anyway, already dreading the answer. "Expecting a fourth?"

Neither of them spoke. They just gave matching nods toward the living room.

Theo groaned inwardly. That floral scent he'd caught earlier, he'd told himself it was the neighbour's garden in bloom. Roses, maybe. But no, it had clung too closely to the hallway, too familiar. It wasn't roses. It was Maggie. His... girlfriend? Ex? Something unlabelled and currently very complicated.

"I really need to take that door off its hinges," he muttered. "Or knock down a wall. Something to stop the constant ambushes."

He stood and walked with all the confidence of a man approaching an enemy trench. Inwardly, his nerves danced in time with a rhythm he hadn't heard since childhood. That itch of vulnerability. Of being seen.

She was facing the window when he entered, dressed in deep violet, the velvet catching the light in slow gradients. A purple headband framed her golden hair. Even her shoes matched. Of course they did.

She turned, and the skirt flared out like a blooming flower. Always with the drama, always curated. Even now.

"Before you say anything," Maggie began, "I want to apologise. For everything. You didn't do anything wrong. I lost control of my emotions, I saw red and... I'm sorry."

"You saw red?" Theo asked, careful with his tone. "As in, you were angry?"

"No," she said quickly, interrupting him with a raised hand. "I meant, that time of the month, blood everywhere. Hormonal chaos."

"Ah." He paused, then blinked. "But... you tried to sleep with me?"

She nodded, completely serious. "Different hormones. They came first. The angry ones took over later."

Theo frowned, as if trying to calculate a formula where the numbers kept switching. "I'm not entirely sure I understand... but I accept your apology."

She stepped forward and wrapped her arms around his neck. He let her. When she leaned in, he met her halfway. The kiss wasn't fiery, it was warm, grounding. The kind that calms instead of ignites.

When they broke apart, he gestured toward the kitchen. "Come on. Let's find out what culinary disaster Ds created for us tonight."

"Of course," Maggie said with a grin.

They walked back into the kitchen. D was ladling thick stew into bowls with the seriousness of a priest at an altar. Al, still acting like the responsible houseguest, was buttering slices of bread with absolute focus, like it was a matter of national security.

The room smelled like broth and fresh herbs. And under it, that familiar perfume again. This time, it didn't set Theo on edge.

Not entirely.

Theo pulled out a chair for Maggie and waited until she was seated before lowering himself into his own. D stepped forward, placing a steaming bowl of stew in front of him with ceremonial care. A moment later, Al slid a plate of buttered bread into the centre of the table with a flourish.

"Thank you," Maggie said, looking between them. "For the meal, and the chance to make it up to Theo."

"You're welcome, milady," Al replied, tipping an imaginary

hat like a court jester in service to romance.

D took the seat opposite Theo, resting his elbows gently on the table's edge. "We don't say grace in this house," he said, casting a glance at Maggie. "But if you do, we're happy to wait."

Theo almost laughed. D loathed anything religious. Once, he'd called it the "most widespread and efficient method of delusion ever invented." But he still offered the choice. That was D all over, disdain with a side of decency.

"Oh no, thank you," Maggie replied with a polite wave. "I lost belief in a higher being years ago. You can dig in, this smells amazing."

"You're most welcome," D said, already halfway to the bottom of his bowl.

"So," Maggie said, tearing a piece of bread and dipping it neatly into her stew, "how was everyone's morning?"

Al raised a hand like a schoolboy. "Yeah, Theo, tell us about that case you worked on this morning."

A fleck of food leapt from his mouth as he spoke. He paused, swallowed hurriedly. "Oops. Sorry."

Theo looked down at his untouched stew. The smell was inviting, rich and warm, spiced with rosemary and something smoky beneath it. "I don't think it's dinner conversation. Might kill your appetite."

"I don't mind," Maggie said, dabbing the corner of her mouth with a napkin. Her eyes held his a moment too long.

Of course she didn't mind. She wanted the details. Wanted to listen. To learn. To watch.

Theo hesitated. Was it paranoia creeping in? Or was it logic finally catching up?

He reached for his spoon, eyes still on her. "Alright. But don't say I didn't warn you…"

Al, however, did not look okay.

He looked better than before, clean-shaven, freshly cut hair slicked back, and wearing one of D's better shirts, even buttoned to the collar. For a moment, he passed as put-together.

But Theo saw it. The pallor rising fast beneath the surface, leeching the colour from Al's skin. It started at his chin and crept upward, climbing toward his hairline like frost spreading across glass. The sweat, which Theo had assumed was from the kitchen heat, now poured from him in torrents. His body began to tremble, subtle at first, then like he'd been dunked in an ice bath.

He was propped on his forearms, elbows digging into the table, head bowed as his mouth worked around a growing flood of saliva.

Theo stood up fast.

"Come on," he said, already reaching for him.

He helped Al to his feet and half-dragged, half-guided him to the small toilet beneath the stairs. The moment Al's head was over the bowl, his body convulsed, and he emptied the contents of his stomach with a guttural, shuddering heave.

D appeared in the doorway a second later, grimacing.

"I've got him," he said, rolling up his sleeves. "You entertain your guest. If it gets worse, I'll shout."

Theo hesitated.

"It's withdrawals," he said quietly. "Delayed onset. They hit harder that way."

D nodded. "Go."

Theo stepped back as D took his place, crouching beside their friend.

He returned to the kitchen.

Maggie was still seated at the table, unphased. She tore

another slice of bread from the plate and dipped it calmly into her stew.

"Is he okay?" she asked, not looking up.

"He's in the worst of it," Theo said, settling back into his chair. "This bit makes or breaks you. If he can ride it out, he'll be clean again. For a while."

Maggie finally looked up. "It's good he has you two." Her tone was gentle. But there was something else in her eyes. Something harder to place.

Theo wasn't sure if it was admiration, or calculation.

"So," Maggie asked, dabbing the corner of her mouth with a napkin, "your morning?"

Theo cleared his throat. "Oh… erm. It was a fight. Looked like one, at least. A lovers' quarrel turned savage. Probably over drugs. But, I think, it was more than that. Two bottles, medicine, maybe, were missing from the scene. They weren't in the wreckage."

"Oh no," she said, spoon halfway to her mouth. "So, you think… they killed each other? Slowly?"

"That's the surface story. But the injuries, placement, patterns, and the room's layout, they tell something else. I think someone else was there. Watched the first blows. Escalated it. Then finished the job and took the drugs."

Maggie lowered her spoon, slowly.

"Are you following any leads?"

Theo shook his head. "Police want this one. Just called me in for the initial sweep. Nothing to chase… yet." He took a bite of his stew. It really was fantastic.

"What about you?" he asked. "How was your morning?"

"Boring, really. Cleaning. Laundry. Some stains are stubborn, you know?" She pushed her empty bowl away, satisfied.

"Compliments to the chef."

A wet, guttural retch echoed from the toilet down the hall.

Theo sighed and nudged his own bowl away, appetite gone.

"Walk?" he offered. "Coffee sounds good right now."

"I'd love to." She smiled, that sly edge to it curling at the corners. "Lead on, Theodore."

They left arm in arm, stepping out into the afternoon air like any couple might, if not for the trail of bloodied mornings they both tried to leave behind.

As they walked along the road, Theo glanced at Maggie. A thought struck him, he knew a lot about her routines, her preferences, her reactions… but not much about her life. He'd assumed too much. Time to fix that.

"So," he began casually, "how's work?"

He kept it open-ended, softening his tone in case she was still volatile from the previous day's clash.

Maggie let out a sigh, her breath turning white in the cool air. "Awful, honestly. I had a shift cancelled again. I do deep cleaning for commercial spaces, usually once a week per client. But if there's a surprise CEO visit, they shut everything down. Rescheduled me for tomorrow though, so… silver lining. Still, it's a hit to the finances."

Theo nodded. "Do you clean anywhere I might know?"

"Probably," she said with a smirk. "I've scrubbed half of London at this point. Offices, kitchens, warehouses. Mum and Dad still hate it. Said I should've gone into finance or law. Apparently, being on the maths team and playing hockey makes you too 'rounded' to settle for bleach and hard work."

She unhooked her arm from his and let their fingers intertwine. Theo squeezed gently, grounding himself in the moment.

"Any siblings?" he asked.

"One. Nick. Older. He moved up to Manchester to start a hauling company. War effort scooped him right up, he transports Spitfire parts now. Brags about it in every letter."

Theo chuckled. "I didn't have siblings to compete with, but there was this neighbour's kid, always being praised for how hard he worked. I got better grades just by showing up, and somehow that made me the lazy one."

She smiled and swung their joined hands between them like a slow pendulum.

"Here we are," she said, releasing his hand with a parting rub along his arm. "Let's get that coffee, and check in on Al. See if he's still riding out the storm."

They stepped into the café, warmth and roasted beans enveloping them like a familiar coat. For a moment, it felt like they'd both left something behind on the street outside, something heavy neither of them had known they were carrying.

7. EVERYONE'S SUSPECT

12:03 14/03/1943
17 Ellington Road, East Hounslow

Theodore Nash had spent the entire morning cross-legged beneath the kitchen table, a bowl of chopped onions and horseradish balanced in his lap. The fumes had done their job early on, tears stung his eyes, his nose ran steadily, but now, four hours in, they were beginning to sting again with a vengeance. The smell had long since passed from irritating to invasive, clinging to his skin and soaking into the fibres of his clothes.

He didn't move. Didn't shift. Didn't blink more than necessary.

From his low vantage point, he stared up at his murder board, the collage of newspaper clippings, photographs, scribbled notes, and pins all weaving a web of obsession above him. Every square inch mattered. Every smudge of ink and tear of paper had purpose. It had to.

The previous victims.

The last one.

The epoxy cube, still held in evidence.

The ropework, expert level, controlled.

The victims' ages, physical states, and social circles.

The Inwood Park Event Centre's logbook.

The unrelated double murder, gruesome, chaotic, but not without echoes.

The ability to drug, bind, lift, suspend, bleed, and disappear.

It all pointed to someone calculated. Someone dangerous.

Strong.

Smart.

Educated.

One step ahead.

Dedicated.

Deceptive.

But were they also... lucky?

Theo frowned. It wasn't unheard of. Killers slipping through cracks in systems. A pattern missed. A detail overlooked. A face too familiar or too ordinary to raise alarm. It was dangerous, he knew, to underestimate someone simply because they didn't match a profile. That was where most investigators failed. That was where victims died.

He leaned his head back against the underside of the table and closed his eyes briefly. He couldn't afford to let this one keep going.

He had to find them, before they claimed another life.

Before they got to Alfie Cartwright.

And then, as if summoned by his thoughts, two sets of feet shuffled slowly into the kitchen.

"So, you slept with her? That's wrong on so many levels," came D's voice, heavy with judgment but undercut by a tone of disbelief.

Theo didn't react. He stayed where he was under the table, trying to tune them out, eyes fixed on the web of clues and half-burnt thoughts on the board above. If he concentrated hard enough, maybe the noise would dissolve back into silence.

"She offered," Al said defensively. "We got high, she passed out."

A beat.

"Even afterwards, when she woke up, she said I could do it again sometime."

D made a sound halfway between a laugh and a groan. A sound reserved for moments when the world felt just a bit too ridiculous to be real. The fridge door swung open with a familiar creak, followed by the clink of glass bottles shifting as D rummaged inside.

Theo identified him by his lighter steps, quiet, precise, like a man avoiding creaky floorboards. Al, by contrast, was dragging one foot slightly, a side-effect of the withdrawal fatigue that weighed him down like wet wool. He stopped just beside the table, and the familiar groan of wood announced his elbows had found purchase.

"So did you?" Theo was surprised at D asking such a question when the answer was obvious.

"Twice," Al added, like he'd won a prize and didn't know what to do with it. "Which brings me back to Theo. He should've just slept with her. She's been good for him. Brought him out of that awkward shell."

"He probably had a reason," D said, voice muffled by the sound of vegetables being tossed onto a counter. "It's only been a week. Maybe he wants to take it slow."

"You can't deny how similar they are, though."

"What? The reason they work is because they're so different. He's calm, collected. She's a wild card, says what she thinks without stopping to breathe." The tap turned on. Running water layered over his words like static. Theo smelled tomatoes, D's usual attempt to make something healthy out of food that shouldn't be messed with.

"I don't mean personalities," Al clarified. "I meant their lives. Dead parents, no siblings, a single friend growing up... wait, have you farted?"

Theo stifled a laugh. Al pulled out a chair and sat down, the scrape of wood sharp against the floorboards. His knees almost colliding with Theo's shoulder.

"Sorry, her parents aren't dead," D said over the water. "They live in Canada. And she's got a sister who works with the royal horses. King George's personal stables, apparently. And no, I haven't."

Theo blinked. That was news.

"Where'd you get that from?" Al chuckled. "You're getting her mixed up with someone else."

"No, she told me. At your party." The tap squealed as D shut it off. "I asked her a few things, had to, for Theo's sake. Gave her the polite version of the inquisition."

"Right. Well, she told me the other day, when you went to make tea, that her parents died when she was twelve , no sister and her best friend ran away to join a commune in Norfolk." Al's voice carried a smug edge. "So, unless her friend has got a teleportation device and a thing for drama, something's off."

D stepped closer. Theo heard the shift of weight, the slow lean against the table's edge.

"You sure you're not confused?" D asked, tone suddenly sharper. "You're not exactly at your most dependable right now."

Al didn't flinch. "Just because I'm sweating out half my organs doesn't mean I've lost my memory. I grew up with Theo. You learn to notice things."

A pause.

"Something I guess you haven't figured out how to do yet."

D's posture stiffened.

"What exactly are you implying?"

Theo decided to intervene before they went too far off topic. He shifted from under the table, rising to his feet with the pungent bowl still in hand. The onions had long since dried at the edges, but the horseradish continued to sting his eyes.

"Go back to what Maggie told you both," he said flatly.

Al jumped, banging his knee hard on the underside of the table. D, caught mid-sentence, threw his arms up with a startled squeal, nearly dropping the tomato he was holding.

"Have you been there the whole time? You almost killed me, you fool," D snapped, one hand clutched to his chest, trying to steady his breathing.

"How much did you hear?" Al asked, wincing as he rubbed his knee, his pale face creased in discomfort.

"Only that you had sex with a girl who slept through it, you think I should have slept with Maggie regardless of reason, and then... I got confused. Which never happens," Theo said, setting the bowl aside and brushing invisible dust from his knees. "It's rare I forget details, and when I do, it's usually childhood memories or something blurred by drug abuse. But I'm sure you both just gave different histories for Mags, including ones that don't match mine."

"Really?" Al paused, his hand slipping away from his knee to clutch his sides. The shaking was starting again. His body rocked subtly, a tremor from deep within.

"Three stories," Theo confirmed.

"So, what's the version she gave you then?" D asked, spinning a chair around and dropping into it backwards, his chin now resting on the curved top rail.

"Mum and dad alive and well. Brother hauling Spitfire parts for the war effort."

There was a silence. Then, Al straightened with effort and gave a small nod.

"Sorry, I'm going to have to excuse myself. I'd kill for a pill or two. These shivers are awful, deep in my bones. Were they this bad for you?"

"Yes," Theo said, his voice quieter now. "It's only awful the once."

He remembered the worst of it, the sensation of crawling out of his own skin, wrapped in threadbare cloth, lying curled on the kitchen floor with bile in his throat and heat prickling at his scalp. The headaches. The silence between retches. The long minutes spent holding on.

"If someone offered me a single pill right now, I'd easily do all of this..." Al gestured to the cluttered wall of notes and photos behind Theo, now lined with strings and scribbled annotations.

Theo raised a single brow.

Al gave a humourless huff and sulked off out of the kitchen, his footsteps dragging, one hand pressed to his ribs.

"No, of course not, he was just joking." D's eyes were fixed on Theo, but the laugh he gave didn't reach his face. His brow remained raised in quiet suspicion.

"He said he would," Theo replied, voice low, like he didn't want the walls to hear it. "What if this is a countdown to his suicide? A last supper, stretched over a week. What if he needed to be around people one final time?"

"Stop making it logical," D snapped. "He's desperate for drugs, he's exhausted. Didn't you feel the same? Didn't you think something just as dark when you were in the thick of it?"

"I did." Theo folded his arms, pacing a short, stilted line across the kitchen tiles. "But I can't help it. I see the pattern, even when I don't want to. He's the right build. Right size. Has the right level of strength to do it. He's been around me long enough, listened to enough of my mad ramblings, to have picked up the methods. If someone were going to snap, it would look just like this. Isolation. Weakness. Precision masked by pain."

D's posture shifted. Defensive now.

"No." The word landed like a full stop. "I've been with him all week. Every hour. No one's come to see him. No one's slipped in or out. I'd have seen it."

Theo narrowed his eyes, lips tightening at the corners. "That's true. You have been with him all week. Growing close. Becoming friendly."

D's expression darkened, his brow furrowed. "What do you mean by that?"

"You said it yourself, you were here the whole time. You could've controlled what I saw. You could've manipulated things, so I'd be the one to ask you to keep watch. Kept me out of the loop while something played out under my nose."

D scoffed and threw up his hands. "You set me on that babysitting job yourself."

"I did," Theo admitted. "But you've spent time around me too. You've listened, picked up my habits, my deductions. You could have learned a thing or two. The way you talk, the way you explain things, hell, even the way you cook, so methodical. That's me. That's my rhythm. You mirror it."

"Now you're being paranoid." D's voice went flat again, but there was a flicker of something else underneath, anger, or maybe hurt. "That's not like you, Theodore."

He turned toward the hallway with a grunt, gesturing dismissively over his shoulder. "I'm going to check on your friend. Make sure he hasn't vomited on my other pair of slippers."

And with that, he was gone.

Theo stood in the silence that followed, the stew's scent still hanging in the air, now mixed with something sharper. Doubt.

He looked around the room, at the shoes near the back door, at the half-open cupboard D had rummaged through, at the half-eaten slice of bread still on Al's plate.

Realising he was still holding onto the pungent bowl of fumes, he set it down on the table.

And then, slowly, he ducked back under the kitchen table.

It wasn't just the space he liked. It was the shift in perspective.

He sat cross-legged once more, the bowl still reeking from above. With the room inverted from this angle, he began to trace the thread again, rewinding timelines, reweighing strengths, and motives, reconsidering every familiar face with just a touch more suspicion.

The list of suspects was growing. And somehow, everyone was on it.

15:36 14/03/1943
17 Ellington Road, East Hounslow

Theo sat hunched over the kitchen table, sleeves rolled past his elbows, a half-drunk cup of tea slowly cooling by his left hand. In front of him, laid out like treasure maps, were his shorthand notes, pages of carefully selected names, dates, and vague job roles from the Event Centre's logbook.

He'd memorised most of it already, but paper helped him visualise patterns. And patterns helped him sleep.

Most of the names were forgettable. Single-time entries, odd surnames that never appeared again. But he wasn't interested in the one-offs. He was searching for the names that showed up more than once, especially around key dates, the days before each murder.

Caterers. Temps. Volunteers. The kind of people who drifted through a place like smoke. Hired for a day, maybe a week, then vanished again.

He glanced down at the open phone book beside him. His finger ran the column like a priest reading from scripture. He'd already marked off half a dozen matches. Now came the fun part.

He reached for the rotary phone on the wall, lifted the receiver, and spun the dial with the calm precision of a man used to lies. He waited for the tone, then cleared his throat and slipped into character.

"Operator, this is Constable Harris from the Southwark Station. I'm hoping to place a local welfare call, routine check-up. Off the record." He pitched his voice deeper, warmer. The kind of voice people wanted to believe.

There was a pause. Then came a giggle he recognised.

"Oh, Theo, you do this every time. You're lucky I like you."

He grinned. "You say that like it's a bad thing, Martha."

"You'll owe me another bottle of sherry."

"Put it on my tab."

Click. The line shifted, connected, began to ring.

The first man answered after two rings. Gruff. Sounded like he was half-asleep or halfway through a hangover.

"Yes?"

Theo slipped into the role again, this time as an event planner following up on freelance records. He asked about a job done three weeks ago, a wedding at the Inwood Centre. The man could barely remember what he ate yesterday.

Definitely not him.

He thanked him and rang off.

The next number, no answer.

The one after that, an overly friendly woman who kept trying to guess who he was based on his voice. She remembered the event clearly, but only because she'd spilled tomato soup on the bride's mother. She didn't strike him as capable of murder. Or epoxy work.

On and on it went.

Every call made the list shorter. Those he couldn't reach, he circled in red and jotted the addresses next to them. One way or another, he'd find out who'd been in that building, who might have slipped under the radar.

He leaned back in the chair, rubbing at the corner of his eye where tiredness had begun to form a dull ache.

He thought of D's words again, calling him paranoid, saying it wasn't like him.

He was right. It wasn't like him. Not to this extent.

Maybe he'd let the stress skew his focus. Maybe he'd spent too long beneath tables with onions and horseradish fumes, building shadows where there weren't any.

He looked to the wall where his suspects were pinned, where a red string had been drawn between Alfie, Darrell, and Maggie, not as culprits, but as question marks.

He reached for the tack that held D's name and removed it. There was no reason to suspect D. Not really. He'd been with Alfie every day. He hadn't so much as stepped out alone.

And Maggie, he paused a moment longer before pulling hers down. Not because of the argument, or the false family details, but because those lies didn't smell like malice.

They smelled like hurt. The kind people wore like perfume to mask something far deeper. She wasn't hiding a motive, she was hiding pain. Trauma. The kind of thing that might take time to explain. If she ever wanted to explain it at all.

And Al... he was spiralling, yes. Withdrawals were crushing

him, but suicidal? No. Al wouldn't have taken Theo's help if he'd already made peace with dying. And he wouldn't have let Theo stay close if he'd meant to cut him out.

Theo removed the line between them and the others. A clean break. No more doubting those his gut told him were safe.

No more second-guessing shadows when the killer was still out there, walking in daylight.

It was time to focus.

The real suspect was still out there.

And Theo intended to find them.

8. TREACHEROUS DISGUISE

14:00 15/03/1943
17 Ellington Road, East Hounslow

Two days left. That thought should have made Theo anxious, but it didn't. Instead, he felt a creeping sense of clarity. The case was about to close, or at least, that's what his gut told him. He wasn't sure how. Nothing tangible had shifted, no puzzle piece had clicked into place with a satisfying snap. But something in the air, some atmospheric pressure only he seemed to feel, told him the end was in sight.

And yet, that gut was contradicting the evidence. In the five days since Alfie's name appeared in the Inwood Park Event Centre's logbook, not a single new person had entered their lives. No strange parcels. No new workers. No one lurking near the house. No rigged pulleys or strange sounds in the attic. No murder weapon tucked in shadows. Nothing.

Theo sat alone in the living room, sunlight cutting a dusty path across the carpet, fingers interlocked beneath his chin. The silence hummed with unsolved riddles. Logic had gotten him this far, and now it was betraying him, because nothing made sense.

He pulled out his notepad, worn at the corners and smudged with ink and thought. Each name he had copied from the stolen logbook, now long handed over to Tucton, was neatly cross-referenced with phone book entries, personal notes, and physical limitations.

Of the six names he'd chased down, not one of them fit.

One woman in a wheelchair, retired from catering three years ago, only kept on the books for legal technicalities.

Two with damaged shoulders, one old rugby injury, the other a broken collarbone from slipping on ice last winter.

A man with advanced arthritis in both knees, walked with a cane and a wince.

A semi-literate teenager who couldn't tell the difference between 'venison' and 'venereal' during their awkward call.

The last was a one-time temp who hadn't worked there since last spring.

None of them could've lifted a body, let alone hoisted one up into the air and orchestrated the brutal display that was becoming the killer's calling card.

Frustrated, Theo leaned back, his gaze catching the edges of the murder board. No red string. Just black lines, tight handwriting, pinned photos, and post-war newspaper clippings. A battlefield of logic. And all of it was pointing in the wrong direction.

He changed tack.

Maybe the killer hadn't signed the logbook at all.

The Event Centre was a public building. That meant government workers could enter without signing the official event logs. People like inspectors, clerical officers, lawyers, or accountants, positions that required presence but didn't warrant scrutiny. Those types rarely left a trace. They didn't get noticed. That made them ideal.

But that introduced a different problem, motive. Why would an accountant murder five unrelated victims? Why would a health inspector go to such elaborate, ritualistic lengths? Unless it wasn't about who the victims were. Maybe it was simply about opportunity. About ego. About getting away with it because they could.

He rubbed at his eyes and tried to picture the logbook again. Every name. Every smudge of pen. The coffee stain covering a few names. The handwriting changing with each person and the mix of red, black and blue ink. Even repeated names, told a story of the way it was written.

Deeper groves for those who are in a rush or irritated that day, the pen hardly touching the paper for more feminine penmanship.

There has to be a name, overlooked, hidden in plain sight.

There.

A.R. Cleaning Services.

It had been there once. A single entry. The name hadn't stood out. Generic. Service industry. Dismissed in the first pass. He remembered glancing over it and assuming it was a background detail, noise, not signal.

But it was the only entry that hadn't aligned to the rest of the staff roster.

Theo sat up straight, heart rate quickening. If someone were to slip in unnoticed, dressed as a cleaner, armed with excuses and keys... it could work. No one would stop a cleaner. Cleaners had access. Cleaners had privacy.

Theo started to think, that was all they needed. A single day once a month to note upcoming events and then find their kill. If no one fitted the bill they could wait it out.

The killer might not have seen Als birthday event at all. His plan to capture the killer was looking less likely to succeed. It had to.

However, cleaners didn't get questioned.

He needed to find out who worked for A.R. Cleaning Services.

That meant digging again, deeper than before.

Theo almost lunged for the phone book, flipping through the pages with the urgency of a man whose answer might vanish if he moved too slow. His finger skimmed the numbers, pausing on the one he needed. A.R. Cleaning Services.

He dialled swiftly. Local number. Good. That meant no operator, no need for greased palms or elaborate favours.

The phone rang twice. A soft click.

"Hello, A.R. Cleaning Services, Angela speaking. How may I help you today?"

The voice was young. Dainty. Sweet in a way that might've seemed disarming if Theo weren't already layering on a different skin.

He became John Haverd, valet to the mythical Mr. Calder, a name that, he hoped, carried the right blend of vague aristocracy and local clout. He deepened his voice, steady and clipped. Just enough to sound both professional and entitled.

"Hello, my name is John Haverd, and I'm calling on behalf of Mr. Calder. I'm sure you're familiar with the name, being a local company."

A pause. "Y... yes, I mean no, sorry," Angela stammered, flustered but polite.

"Well," Theo continued, "Mr. Calder requires a fortnightly cleaning service of his townhouse. I'd like to inquire about your availability and pricing."

"Ah, well, sir, that would depend on whether the townhouse is small or large. Could you tell me how many rooms, including bathrooms?"

"Thirteen," Theo replied. "And another single-room building off the main house."

There was a faint whistle. "That's quite a size, sir. For something of that scale, the pricing would be... three pounds, three shillings, and nine-and-a-half pence per visit. Would that be suitable for Mr. Calder?"

"Perfectly," Theo said with smooth assurance. "Now, do you perform the cleaning yourself, or do you employ a team? Mr. Calder is very particular about who enters the property."

"Oh, it's just me, sir. But for larger jobs, I do bring in help through the agency."

"Do you select your own team, or are they assigned?"

"Afraid it's whoever's available. Labour's short these days, what with the war and all, God bless them. The agency rotates staff quickly now. I'm lucky to get more than three assistants at once, and that's rare. So, for a house that size, you'd be looking at two to three days depending on how many they send."

Theo let the silence linger for a beat. Then, "Understood. I'll speak with Mr. Calder and ring you back shortly with his answer."

"Of course, sir. Thank you kindly."

He hung up.

Theo groaned, low and tight in his throat. Another lead reduced to dust. Another brick wall rising in front of him, stone-faced and smug. Every trail he followed seemed to double back, dead-end, or dissolve into fog.

It was like chasing ghosts with footprints that vanished the moment he looked down.

The cleaning service was another dead end, Angela wasn't the killer. And if she'd brought help, it had been faceless, nameless, agency fodder, shuffled in and out too fast to remember, let alone trace.

Frustration clawed at the edges of his mind, scraping with impatient fingers. He could almost feel his own sanity shaking him by the collar, demanding results. Not just for the victims. For Alfie. For himself.

He pressed his palms into his eyes and exhaled through clenched teeth.

He had two days. Two. The killer had waited long enough before striking again, any longer and Alfie would be next. And Theo couldn't afford another brick wall.

He needed a window. A crack. A splinter in the structure.

Something he'd missed.

Something small.

15:00 15/03 1943
17 Ellington Road, East Hounslow

Theo pressed a hand against the wall and pushed himself up from the kitchen floor, legs aching from too long folded beneath him. The lingering frustration from yet another dead-end call tugged at his thoughts. He needed to reset. To go back to the beginning. If Alfie Cartwright was the next intended victim, then Alfie was also the clearest starting point.

He stepped out of the kitchen and into the living room.

For a moment, no longer than a breath, his heart collapsed into his chest.

His father was on the sofa, or rather, draped upside down across it in a grotesque pose: his back arched unnaturally over the seat, head dangling toward the floor, chin to the sky. A crimson line curved under his jaw, blood running backwards up his face, soaking into his hair, and dripping rhythmically into a perfect circle on the carpet.

Theo blinked. Hard.

When his vision refocused, his father was gone. Alfie was there instead, curled strangely, hanging half-off the cushions like he'd slid down in his sleep. His robe bunched around his midsection, and his breath came in shallow, uneven pulls. The pool of blood was gone. Only the usual speckling of ash from the fireplace marked the floor.

Theo rubbed the tired from his eyes with the back of his hand and sighed.

Al stirred, righting himself slowly and curling into a ball, knees tucked up to his chest. He looked pale, sweat clinging to his forehead, but the worst of the shakes seemed to have passed for now.

D was sat in his usual chair, eyes following Theo closely.

Theo pulled the footstool around and sat directly in front of Al. "I need to ask you a few questions. It's important. Has anyone new come into your life lately? Anyone old reconnected? A familiar face? A delivery man? the postman?"

Al squinted at him. "I haven't been anywhere, Theo. Not in the past week, not since you took me in. No one's come to see me except you two." His voice was raspy. "Unless someone's sneaking in at night to watch me vomit, I've been mostly here. D can confirm."

D raised a brow. "I'm not his jailor, but yes. He hasn't exactly had the energy to go for walks."

Theo looked from one to the other. "So, no contact with any of the catering staff, cleaners, nothing like that?"

Al shook his head, Theo noted the instant regret in his choice of movement, instead of words.

"He's exhausted," D interrupted. "Can't you see he's in no state to play interviewee right now?"

"I know, but..."

"But nothing. This can wait."

Theo opened his mouth to argue, but Al sat up suddenly, holding the arm of the couch until the headrush passed.

"Let's have a drink," Al said. "One drink. I need to feel human for a bit. I need to feel like I'm not dying."

Theo hesitated. D was already nodding.

"I'll even break out your good stuff," Al said with a grin that was more hollow than hopeful.

Theo sighed. He remembered how much it had helped, that single night D had sat with him, cracked jokes, shared a bottle, reminded him he wasn't alone in the fog. And Al... he deserved that too.

"All right," Theo said quietly. "One drink."

Al disappeared into the hallway and returned with three dusty bottles of beer. He handed one to each of them, the labels faded and peeling.

They drank in silence for a while, the soft ticking of the hallway clock the only sound between them. The living room was dim, the fireplace long since gone cold, but the company made the chill bearable.

D leaned back in his chair, stretching his legs. "You know," he said casually, "I once tried to make beer myself. During the last sugar ration."

Al groaned. "Please tell me you didn't use beetroot."

"Worse," D said. "Radishes. I thought the peppery kick would be a selling point."

Al gave a quiet laugh. "And what happened?"

"I poisoned a vicar," D said with a proud nod. "Only mildly. He hallucinated the Second Coming in the middle of a christening."

Al let out a wheezing laugh that turned into a cough. "You're a menace."

"But a memorable one."

The laughter faded naturally, like a warm breeze passing through. Theo leaned back and watched Al cradle his bottle loosely in his hands, cheeks flushed, chest rising and falling steadily. His friend looked, if only briefly, peaceful.

Al took another sip, then glanced at Theo. "Thanks, mate. For putting up with me. I know I'm not exactly charming right now and i'm sorry."

"You've never been charming," Theo said, managing a faint smile. "But you're still here. That counts for something."

Al grinned and raised his bottle again. "To getting clean."

D followed suit. "To bad beer and worse company."

Theo touched his bottle to theirs. "To friends."

And in that moment, to Theo at least, it felt like everything might finally turn a corner.

9. CONSEQUENTIAL RELAPSE

13:25 16/03/1943
17 Ellington Road, East Hounslow

Theo woke in disarray. A sour patch of drool soaked through the side of his cheek, matting his hair into the damp pillow. His ear felt wet. Uncomfortably so. The sharp tang of bile stung at the back of his throat, and his tongue felt like he'd been sucking on copper nails all night.

The room was dark, but his skull throbbed behind his eyes in waves, like his brain was trying to claw its way out. He reached a hand out, half expecting to find someone next to him, some evidence of a night of blissful sin, but the bed was cold. He was still dressed. Shoes and all.

It was the clothes that got him. Something about waking fully clothed in bed dredged up an old memory: a piss-stained mattress on the upper floor of some forgotten squat house. His first real overdose scare. Still half-high, heart galloping like a racehorse, legs twitching, mind fogged in spirals of regret. That kind of shame made its home in the bones.

"No," he whispered to himself. "No. That was years ago."

But the aching throb in his limbs, the weight pressing on his chest, the dizziness that threatened to suck him down through the floor, it all felt too damn familiar.

He sat up fast. Mistake.

His stomach lurched, and he fought it, breathing slow, pushing the taste down. He blinked hard and forced his body to swing his legs over the edge of the bed. He sat there, hunched forward, hands gripping the edge of the mattress like it would steady the tilt of the world.

Then it clicked.

The beer.

Last night. The living room. D. Al. A few bottles. Just enough to celebrate. Nothing outrageous. No spirits. Just beer.

Theo stood, a little faster this time, and the room tilted again, like the floor had been knocked off kilter. His foot clipped the leg of the nightstand, and he stumbled toward the door, catching himself with a hand against the wall. The wallpaper felt hot against his skin. Everything felt hot.

By the time he reached the stairs, sweat had broken out across his brow, trickling into his eyes. His stomach rolled again, violently, and he didn't even make it down the first three steps.

Theo buckled forward, grabbing the banister with one hand, the other pressed tight against his stomach as it clenched with volcanic urgency. His knees hit the carpeted steps hard, teeth rattling on impact. It was all he could do to lean sideways and away from the railing before his body gave up the fight.

He vomited, hard.

The first wave was violent, acidic, painted in browns and yellows. It hit the stairs and splashed forward, oozing over the lip of the next step down. He coughed, gagged, and choked again as the second heave came, less fluid now, more convulsion than purge. It splattered messily down the stairwell, tracing a sickening stream like a muddy river breaking through a dam.

Theo groaned, coughing bile, drool, and curses all at once.

His vision blurred, more from the sting of bile in his nose than any tears, though they welled too. He wiped his sleeve across his mouth and crawled another two steps down on trembling limbs, but it wasn't over. His stomach twisted again, and he retched a third time, this one less about contents and more about punishment, dry, wrenching spasms that left his back aching and his throat raw.

The stream of vomit now laced the stairwell from mid-landing to the bottom, thick, yellowish sludge pooling like a grotesque slipstream headed straight for the front door. It glistened in the early light, reflecting a nauseating sheen on the hallway walls.

Theo spat, twice, and forced himself upright again. The world tilted cruelly, but he steadied, blinking back the haze.

He staggered into the hallway.

The air stank, part his own doing, part... something else. Something was off.

The kitchen door was half-open. That was wrong.

The drawer, where they kept medicine, hung open, its contents gutted. That was very wrong.

Theo's heart began to pick up pace, a dull thump that echoed in his skull. The fridge door was ajar. Two chairs were toppled. The table had been shoved aside, skewed on its axis. Scrape marks trailed the floor as if someone had moved it in a hurry.

A growing hollowness opened in his chest.

He turned to the living room.

Gone.

The telly, gone. Just an empty gap on the stand, the cables still dangling like severed veins.

He spun, staggered toward the pantry, pulled aside the loose panel above the dry goods.

Ration tabs, still there. The coin stash tucked in the ceramic sugar tin, untouched. The emergency bills behind the row of lentils and salt, present. Even D's stash was safe and sound inside an empty tin of instant coffee.

Why take the TV and leave everything else?

Theo's gut twisted.

Al.

It had to be Al.

He drugged them, drugged him. Theo had barely touched the beer. Just a bottle and a half. But it was enough. A subtle taste, bitterness that hadn't registered at the time. Something fast-dissolving. Al must've slipped it in when Theo had stepped out to piss or take a call. And D, he'd barely been drinking, had he?

A fresh stab of fear pushed Theo forward.

D.

He turned and thundered back up the stairs, feet slipping once in the mess of his own sick. He caught himself on the banister, boot scraping the wall with a loud, ugly screech.

He slammed into the hallway, sprinted to D's room.

And stopped.

Dead still.

D lay sprawled on the floor, half-crumpled, head turned awkwardly to one side. His mouth was open, too wide. From it, a slow line of vomit trailed down his cheek and across the floorboards, pale and foamy. His eyes were closed, chest unmoving.

"No," Theo breathed. His stomach seized again, but he fought it.

He dropped to his knees, grabbing D by the shoulder.

"D?"

No response.

He tilted his friend back. D's lips were tinged blue. His jaw slack. His skin was clammy and cold at the edges, but warm, too warm, at the centre. And the pool of vomit was fresh.

Not gone. Not yet.

Theo rolled him with sudden urgency, flipping D to his side, watching as the rest of the trapped sick spilled from his mouth in thick, wet globs. It stained the floor, a foul halo beneath his head. D coughed once, a twitch, a spasm, but no breath followed.

"Shit."

Theo didn't hesitate. He flipped D flat on his back again and leaned over him.

No breath. No heartbeat he could feel.

He scanned the room. Something. He needed to get someone's attention.

His eyes locked on the wooden model ship that sat on D's desk, an old, polished thing with reinforced edges and decorative brass detailing.

Theo lunged for it, grabbed it in both hands, and hurled it at the window with everything he had.

The glass shattered. The ship sailed into the street like a cannonball, taking curtains and shards with it. The crash echoed through the block, a sound designed to summon alarm.

He turned back.

Dropped to his knees.

Placed his hands on D's chest.

And began to push.

He began compressions.

One. Two. Three. Four.

The heel of his hand slammed into D's chest with precision born not of training but desperation. Thirty rapid compressions, two breaths. Again. Theo's arms shook. Sweat ran into his eyes.

The slick of vomit and panic made the floor treacherous beneath him, but he didn't stop. Couldn't.

Five. Six. Seven.

D's head lolled with each press, his limbs bouncing slightly on the floor. Theo gritted his teeth and pushed harder, counting in time with the thud of his own heartbeat.

"Twelve. Thirteen. Fourteen…"

He tilted D's head, pinched his nose, and blew.

Once. Again.

No reaction.

Back to compressions.

"Come on, D," he growled through clenched teeth. "You are not going out like this."

Nineteen. Twenty. Twenty-one.

Every rib felt like it might crack. Every push a prayer disguised as pressure. Theo's vision blurred, not from tears, but from the sheer focus it took to keep going.

Twenty-eight. Twenty-nine. Thirty.

Another breath. Another. Still no movement.

Theo hesitated, panic swelling, but no. That window smash would've drawn attention. Help might be on the way. He just had to keep going. Long enough for D to come back. Long enough for someone to burst in. Long enough.

He reset his hands and pressed again. Faster this time.

Thirty compressions. Two breaths.

Then again.

And again.

His shoulders screamed. His back spasmed. His knees were slick with vomit and sweat. And still he pushed.

Theo's voice cracked with each number now. "Thirty-four... Thirty-five..."

His arms moved like pistons. There was no room for hope or dread, only rhythm. Only pressure. Only faith that somewhere, just beneath the surface, D was listening. Fighting.

At the forty-first compression, D jolted.

It was small. Almost nothing.

Then a ragged cough exploded from his mouth, thick and wet and horrifyingly alive. More sick spewed out onto the floor, splashing against Theo's thigh.

Theo flinched back on instinct but didn't move far. He hovered close, watching as D took another breath, a shallow, sucking gasp.

Then another.

And another.

Theo collapsed backward, landing hard on his arse, arms limp, chest heaving.

He watched D roll slightly to his side, eyes fluttering but not quite open, and for the first time since waking, Theo allowed himsel two broken words:

"Thank-fuck."

15:45 16/03/1943
17 Ellington Road, East Hounslow

Theo sat hunched over on the sofa, elbows planted on his knees, head cradled in his hands. The quiet of the house gnawed at him. The air stank faintly of sweat, antiseptic, and sick. While the paramedics had worked on D, He'd scrubbed at the dried vomit until the floorboards splintered his knuckles, but he couldn't get the smell out of his head, or the guilt.

His fingers dug into his hair. The familiar ache was

there again, deeper than physical pain, more insidious. That whispering thirst. The sharp, scratchy edge of want. Wanting more. Needing more. It was just noise at first, but it had shape now. Teeth. Claws.

Drugs. His body was screaming for them. He could feel it in his molars, in the throb behind his temples, in the twitch of his leg as it bounced restlessly. Every nerve ending was jittering with need.

He'd been spiked. He knew that. And yet part of him didn't care. Part of him was grateful for the hit. That terrified him more than anything.

"I failed to stop the next murder," he muttered, voice raw.

"Not yet."

The voice made him jerk upright. D stood in the doorway, bent double like an old man, one hand pressed tight against his ribs. He dragged himself toward the armchair and collapsed into it with a wince, teeth gritted against the pain.

Theo's throat tightened. He didn't know whether to speak or cry.

"You look like shit," D said, his voice papery and strained.

"I could say the same. How the hell are you standing?"

D gave a half-smile, half-grimace. "Thanks to you, I guess. They said you saved my life. Barely bruised some ribs in the process. Guess you missed the sweet spot. Good thinking, getting the attention of the officers outside, shame about my ship though."

Theo scoffed, more of a breath than a laugh. "They give you anything?"

"Water and codeine. I'm living the dream."

Silence lapsed between them for a beat. Then Theo's voice returned, flat and dark. "If I see Al again, I'll kill him."

D watched him carefully. "No, you won't."

"You didn't see what he did. What he nearly..." Theo broke off, stood suddenly, pacing. "He drugged us. Robbed us blind. Took the telly. The food. He nearly killed you, D."

"I'm aware." D's voice was low. "But he's not thinking straight. You remember how that feels. You think you didn't scare the shit out of a few people back in the day? You weren't exactly charming."

Theo turned, fists clenched. "That was different. I never..."

"You nearly died," D cut in. "Three times. I was there, remember? I cleaned you up. I dragged you to cold baths. I held your damn head out of the toilet."

Theo sagged. The fight drained out of him.

They sat in silence again, heavier now. D shifted in the chair with a grunt.

"You've changed," he said after a moment. "You've been different since Maggie."

Theo's head snapped up. "What?"

"Since you met her. You're... softer. More open. Less 'brooding genius', more 'saviour of the damned.'" D gave a weak smirk. "It suits you."

Theo turned away, running both hands over his face. "Yeah. I guess. But she's not part of this. I need to focus. One more day. One more murder."

"Not necessarily," D said quietly.

"What do you mean?"

"You said it yourself. Al's the next target. You've got one more day to stop it."

Theo frowned. "I don't even know if I want to."

"You don't mean that."

"I'm not sure anymore," Theo said, voice hollow. "Maybe I want to stop the killer. Not necessarily save the victim."

D didn't answer. He just looked at him with that same calm patience he'd always had. The look that meant he knew Theo was full of shit and would wait for him to admit it.

Then a thought.

A spark.

Theo turned. "What did you say just now?"

"I said you've got one more day to…"

"No. Before that. About Maggie."

D blinked. "I said she changed you. Since meeting her."

Theo's brain flipped through pages like a file cabinet ablaze. Images, words, moments. Maggie showing up at the party. Maggie always knowing where to find him. Maggie slipping perfectly into place.

"Al's party," Theo said. "She was there. She barely knew me then. At Inwood. You called and told her it was a birthday party."

D's brow furrowed. "Yeah, but that's…"

"No. Think. Think. She's always been one step too close. Too convenient."

"You think Maggie's the killer?"

"I think…" Theo faltered. "I think it's a better idea than Al wanting to kill himself."

The room went cold.

Theo ran to the evidence board, yanked down pages, notes, sketches. Searched for connections, for slips, for gaps.

"Maggie," he muttered. "Maggie Shaw. No verifiable background. Conflicting family stories. False leads."

He stormed through the house like a man possessed. To the spare room. The attic. The basement. Tearing open drawers, checking walls, feeling for loose panels. Looking for tools, rope, syringes, hooks.

Nothing.

He turned the living room inside out, digging under cushions, flipping rugs. Nothing.

It wasn't here.

Another dead end.

But this time, he wasn't giving up.

Not now. Not with one day left.

10. THE HUNT

17:00 16/03/1943
17 Ellington Road, East Hounslow

Theo stood in the hallway, staring at the battered old map he'd unfolded on the side table.

A decision lay before him, one he wasn't eager to make. The faded lines of East Hounslow traced beneath his fingertips: familiar streets, broken alleyways, pockets of memory scattered like scars across the page.

The parts of town where he used to live, no, not live. Haunt.

Where the worst of him once prowled. Where days bled into nights in a fog of sweat and sickness and chemicals that dulled the brightness of a mind too fast for its own good.

He could still taste it if he let himself.

But the clock was ticking now.

Two days. No, One. Less than that, after what's left of today.

And Al was already bait in the water.

Theo drew a slow breath and folded the map again. His hands moved with precision but his mind... it flickered. Just for a moment. Images he didn't want dark stairwells, piss-stained mattresses, faces blurred by withdrawal. And Al, thinner, dirtier, but still there. In every room back then. Peddler. Supplier. Friend? Not anymore. But not enemy, either.

A choice had to be made. If Al was missing, not at the house, then there was only one place he'd go: back into the filth. The people, the places, the life Theo had clawed out of years ago. The old circuit of hiding holes and drug dens scattered across the south side of the borough.

Theo rolled his shoulders back, set the map aside. Time to go hunting.

Footsteps behind him, soft, slippered, then D appeared in the doorway, arms folded across his chest, a mug of tea in one hand.

"You look like you're ready to tear the world down," D said, voice hoarse from sleep. "Where are you off to?"

Theo reached for his coat. "South quarter."

D blinked. "That's not the answer. You're not chasing scraps down there."

Theo didn't respond right away. He adjusted his collar, straightened the lapels. Little rituals to anchor himself.

D watched him. "You're going to the places you used to go, aren't you?"

A pause.

"Yes," Theo said simply. "If he's gone, that's where he'll be."

D rubbed the back of his neck. "Dangerous crowd now, even worse than it used to be. You know that. If he's sunk that low again... he might not want to be found."

Theo gave the smallest shrug. "He's going to be found. And I'm going to be the one who does it."

D sighed heavily, leaning against the wall. "Why do you even care anymore?"

Theo stopped in the act of putting on his gloves. He didn't answer for a moment.

"Because once," he said, voice quiet but certain, "he was the one who gave me the first pill. When my head was screaming too fast to breathe. When I thought my own mind would tear itself apart. He offered me silence."

A thin smile crossed his lips, bitter and fleeting.

"Thought I was clever back then. A genius." He shook his head. "Didn't realise how broken I was."

D was silent now, watching him.

Theo went on, voice steadier.

"It wasn't until my parents were murdered that I pulled myself out of that filth. Sobered. Focused. With your help, then I used this," he tapped his temple..."to chase the bastard who killed them. The one we're chasing now."

D's gaze softened a touch. He set the mug down.

"You're sure about this?" he asked quietly.

Theo nodded once. "The pattern's holding. Al's next."

D ran a hand down his face. "You want me to call Radcliffe? Get more eyes out?"

Theo pulled open the door, glancing back over his shoulder.

"You'll do the right thing," he said, already moving.

And then he was gone, boots thudding down the steps, long coat snapping in the wind.

It was only after the door had shut behind him that Theo noticed.

The police outside, gone.

No stationed car. No familiar figures loitering at the corner, pretending not to watch.

The street was empty.

His stomach twisted.

Why were they gone?

Either way, D stood alone in the hallway now.

And the house was unguarded.

17:28 16/03/1943

Ivy Road, South Hounslow

Ivy Road hadn't changed.

If anything, it had curdled further with time, like something left too long in the summer sun. The narrow street wound south from the old bus depot, skirting the edges of Hounslow's forgotten quarters. The sort of place the council pretended didn't exist, the sort of place polite folk didn't mention in conversations.

But Theo knew it well.

He tightened his coat against the wind, shoulders hunched as he approached the mouth of the alleyway. Ivy Road's filth was familiar, old chip papers caught in doorways, a fractured bottle twinkling green in the gutter, a woman's torn scarf pinned beneath a loose brick. The air smelt of piss, diesel, and stale sweat.

Half a dozen shapes loitered near the alley entrance, young men mostly, in mismatched jackets, eyes like small black pits. They were draped on the railings, sat on doorsteps, or shifting between invisible lines of territory. They clocked him immediately. A sharp glance, a muttered word, a ripple through the group.

Theo didn't falter. He knew the dance.

He kept his pace steady, his face unreadable. Inside though, a different story. The closer he got to that alley, the heavier the memory dragged at him.

Alfie. That first time.

Too fast. Everything had always been too fast, his mind ran on rails the rest of the world couldn't see. Words tripped, thoughts collided, his tongue too slow to keep up. Anger and frustration bleeding through the cracks until Al, grinning, had offered that first small paper packet.

"Just take the edge off, mate. Trust me."

It had worked. Too well. And the nights that followed...

Theo pushed the memories back. Now wasn't the time.

He reached the alley and stepped inside. The buildings on either side leaned inwards, heavy with soot and grime, graffiti scrawled in crude shapes. Bottlecaps littered the ground. The first few feet were damp, the kind of moisture that never quite dried. Further in, the space narrowed, a choke point where business used to happen.

It was empty now.

Theo scanned the dim stretch ahead.

Behind him, footsteps.

Soft at first, but deliberate. Someone had peeled off from the group by the entrance and followed him in.

Theo didn't turn straight away. He waited until the man was close enough to make the crunch of gravel underfoot distinct, then slowly, carefully, turned to face him.

Late twenties maybe, dark coat, flat cap pulled low. Thin face. Gaunt eyes. The sort of man the streets had already half-consumed.

"Alright mate," the man said, not quite a threat but edged enough to test the air.

"I'm looking for someone," Theo replied, voice level. "Had some dealings here earlier this night. Would be an old regular returning for more. Pale, desperate, something about him would stand out."

The man sniffed, eyes flicking down Theo's coat. "Lots of folk come through here. Depends on what you're offering."

Theo reached into his pocket and withdrew a folded note. The feel of it against his fingers sent an involuntary shiver through him. Too close to old habits. His thumb brushed the edge of the paper, and his gut twisted. For a moment, just a heartbeat, he felt it again: the thirst. The want. The old itch beneath the skin.

He pushed it down and held the note out.

The man plucked it quick, eyes darting over his shoulder, then tucked it away. "Yeah... I saw him. Tall lad, pale, bit rough round the edges. That your boy?"

Theo gave a small nod.

"Sold him a bit of gear. Paid with a telly and some ration stamps. Must've been desperate. Didn't hang about after."

"Where'd he go?"

A shrug. "Didn't say. Took off fast."

Theo narrowed his eyes but didn't press. No point. The man was already shifting his weight, eager to be done with this chat.

"Appreciate the honesty," Theo said, voice flat.

The man gave a small smirk. "Pleasure doing business."

Theo turned and made his way back to the street, the man fading into the shadows behind.

As he emerged into the weak daylight of Ivy Road, a sour taste flooded his mouth.

One more brick in the wall. No location. No new names.

And still one day left.

He didn't slow. There were more places to visit, old haunts. Each one a fresh risk, not just to his life... but to what little peace he'd clawed back from the past.

18:04 16/03/1943
Chatsworth Crescent, East Hounslow

Chatsworth Crescent looked the same as ever.

Three houses stood hollow-eyed in the row, abandoned, boarded here and there, but not enough to keep the regulars out. The street was otherwise lived-in, curtains twitching, dogs barking distantly, children's chalk scrawls half-washed away on the cracked pavement.

Theo pulled his coat tighter. The air tasted faintly metallic here, old pipes, decay, something cloying in the back of the throat.

He approached slowly.

Even before he reached the broken gate of Number 37, a shape detached from the shadows, a man weaving slightly as he moved, arms outstretched.

"Theo!" The voice was a slur, but thick with familiarity. "Bloody hell, mate, long time, eh?"

It was Tom.

Gaunt face, wild hair, eyes glassy. He half-staggered toward Theo with an open, drunken grin. "Didn't think I'd see you here again. You look... sharp. Fancy one?" He fumbled in his coat pocket and produced a small pill, pinched between dirty fingers.

Theo's stomach coiled at the sight. His fingers itched to reach for it, an old, instinctive twitch, but he kept them still. Focus. Mission first.

"Not tonight, Tom," Theo said quietly, voice tight. "I'm looking for someone."

Tom tilted his head, swaying in place. "Shame. Party's about to start. Real good batch this time. Bit of fun, eh? You used to love it..."

Theo forced the memory back, clearing his throat. "Have you seen Alfie? Tonight?"

Tom frowned, squinting. "Al? No... Not tonight." He turned, raising his voice down the street. "Audrey!"

A figure down the way looked up, Audrey, in little more than scraps of clothing that barely met decency. She leaned against a post, smoking lazily, hips swaying with practiced rhythm.

Tom grinned. "She'd know. Al always had a soft spot, y'know? Big spender when he came by."

Theo didn't react, though the old stories flickered in his mind, Al's boasting after a high, the women, the blurred lines between pleasure and oblivion.

He took a breath and approached Audrey.

He approached her slowly, boots crunching glass and grit underfoot. Audrey leaned in the lamplight, hollow cheeks, red lips painted wide, eyes rimmed dark but bright with life, of a kind.

"Well, well," she purred, a low, throaty sound. "If it isn't Mister Nash himself. Been an age, love."

She blew out a slow stream of smoke, watching him through the curl of it. "What's brought you back to this side of things? Fancy a lie down with me, for old time's sake?" Her smile curved, suggestive but knowing.

"I'm looking for Al," Theo said, voice level, gaze steady. "Seen him tonight?"

Audrey let the cigarette hang between two fingers, considering. "Mmm... can't say I have. Not for a bit now. Shame, too, he always tipped nice."

She stepped closer, a shift in her weight that sent her thin dress sliding against her frame. "But you..."

She reached out, fingers brushing lightly against his sleeve, a teasing stroke. "You could come in. Do the things we used to do. You always liked my lap... always looked so peaceful."

Her tone dipped lower. "Maybe you need some loving from Audrey tonight. You look tense."

Theo's throat tightened.

The images flared, him, half-gone on the floor of that dark room, head resting in her lap, voices blending in soft nonsense while time slipped away. Comfort, of a kind. False, but deep. A needle poised in memory. That was the pleasure he'd taken from her, not the kind she first offered, and he politely refused, but the strange therapy that followed. Nights spent in tangled talk, the lull of her fingers through his hair, the world outside forgotten.

He swallowed hard. "Not tonight."

A slow pout teased her lips. "Suit yourself, love. But doors always open. You know that."

He gave a brief nod and a small smile, turning away before old comforts snagged their hooks too deep.

It wasn't all bad. But time to move on.

19:23 16/03/1943
Sidmouth Avenue, Spring Grove

The last place.

He dreaded it.

It had taken the better part of an hour to cross town, stopping to check a handful of other old spots, behind shuttered shops, down crooked alleyways behind defunct bus shelters. Each one empty, silent, haunted only by wind and the occasional rustle of unseen vermin.

Now he stood before the carcass of a half-built structure on Sidmouth Avenue, a mid-construction project left to rot when funds ran dry. Concrete floors laid bare to the elements, skeletal beams reaching upward, wrapped in shadows. It had been one of his own crash sites, when he knew the high would be long and brutal. When he wanted to disappear from the world entirely.

He crept inside.

Glass crunched beneath his boots, bottles, syringes,

wrappers, the debris of human wreckage.

He didn't call out. Didn't need to. The place smelled of desperation, of old sweat and sharp chemicals. Someone was here.

Theo rushed through the half constructed skeletal structure, checking each room, looking for a humanoid lump in the floor.

There, second floor, tucked behind a half-finished wall of drywall and wooden supports, a figure curled in the shadows. A woman. Frail, almost sunken into the floor, long hair tangled around thin arms.

Theo's heart lurched.

Miriam.

Of course.

She'd been there in his darkest days. Not a dealer. Not a user in the same way. Just... someone who mothered the broken ones. Held him when the crash went wrong, when the night got cold or the high turned black. She'd saved him from choking more than once.

She stays here to protect the fallen. He always respected her for that.

He approached quietly, crouching.

"Miriam," he said softly, touching her shoulder. "Miriam, wake up."

She stirred, groaning, eyes fluttering open. Recognition dawned, weak but genuine.

"Theo..." her voice cracked, paper-thin. "You... you alright, love?"

"Looking for someone. Al, Alfie Cartwright. You remember him, yeah?"

She nodded, eyes clearer now, pulling herself upright with a wince.

"Al... not seen him, not this week. Not here." She paused, frowning as if trying to recall. "He was talkin'... last I saw him. About a new spot. Said he'd found a place more 'private.' Safer, like."

Theo's pulse quickened. "Where?"

She blinked slowly, lips dry and cracked. "Old apartment complex... up on Whitton Road. Down past the rail arches."

That was enough.

He pressed a five-pound note into her palm without thinking. "Thank you."

Then he was on his feet, bolting back through the crumbling frame of the building. Into the street.

It was late now. The town had settled into its hush. The few souls still out, drunks, vagabonds, night-shifters, watched him sprint by with wide, spooked eyes. Theo didn't care. He shoved past where he had to, dodging shadows, boots striking hard against the pavement.

He had gone full circle, Ivy Road branched off of Whitton Road.

He should have deduced Al wouldn't go that far. He was lazy after all.

He had a lead finally. No more brick wall, that is, if Al really is there.

Al had to be there. The timing was too close. Too damn close.

He turned sharply onto Whitton Road, the breath burning in his chest, when,

A voice, sharp and behind him:

"Nash! What do you think you're doing?!"

Theo skidded, half-turning mid-stride.

There, coat half-buttoned, stood Wallace Tucton. Face flushed from the chase, breath misting in the chilly air,

11. PARENTAL GUIDANCE

20:03 16/03/1943
Whitton Road, South Hounslow

Theo skidded to a stop, boots scraping on wet stone. His chest heaved from the sprint and adrenaline still flooded his veins. Tucton stood in the middle of Whitton Road, coat thrown over a half-tucked shirt, hair dishevelled, steam rising faintly from him in the cold.

They faced each other like a pair of gunslingers. Neither speaking, both catching their breath.

Theo broke the silence first. "What the hell are you doing here?"

Tucton raised both brows, exasperated. "You've got a damn cheek, Nash. I was about to ask you the same thing."

Theo blinked. "I don't have time for this."

"You'd better make time," Tucton shot back. "Your shadow called it in, said you bolted from the house like a man possessed. After what happened this morning, Radcliffe had me checking known slums. Thought you might be out here doing something stupid."

That gave Theo a pause. He could hear the genuine concern under Tucton's gruff tone. The man wasn't here on orders, not fully. He was here on instinct. Friend or not, it was a risk for a copper to come alone this deep at night.

"I'm not here for that," Theo said, voice low. "I'm chasing him."

Tucton frowned. "Who?"

Theo hesitated, only for a second. Then he decided. Sod it. The man was out here on his own, going off gut, risking reputation and more. He deserved the truth. Maybe he could even help.

"The Vampire Killer."

Tucton's eyes widened. "You're joking."

"I'm not."

"The file's still cold. Radcliffe thinks it's stalled. You've been off the grid for days. Remember that double-homicide? Forensics got back , the drugs found in both victims blood was barbiturates. We think that's what the killer stole from there. Also traces were found in the most recent victims bloodwork too."

"Because I'm still working it," Theo shot back. "And I'm closer than any of you think. So the double homicide is connected it was a rushed kill, a supply run. Maggie must have visited me to create an alibi around that time, as well as scope out Al. "

Tucton processed that. "Christ, Nash... you're serious."

Theo gave a sharp nod. "One day left. Al's in danger. The next victim. I'm trying to stop it. Although, I'm starting to believe we don't have one more day. I think it's tonight. If I was the Vampire Killer, tonight has worked out beautifully. Al running out of the protective net, disappearing on his own and seeking oblivion. Poetry in motion"

Tucton paced a step, glanced around the street. "You know... you're a bloody lunatic."

Theo shrugged. "Takes one to catch one. Where did the officers on watch disappear to today? I noticed no one watching."

Tucton gave Theo a hard stare, "With Al already slipping past them in the night, there was no need for the watch, they are patrolling looking for a man of Alfie's description. Radcliffe agreed on the tactic."

Silence stretched again between them, but it wasn't hostile anymore. There was understanding there now, grudging respect.

"Alright," Tucton said. "What's the plan?"

Theo's lips twitched, just slightly. "Plan is... I go in there." He jabbed a thumb toward the looming tenement block up ahead. "You get backup, then follow me up."

"Sounds about right," Tucton smirked. "I'll cover you, since you're clearly off your rocker."

Theo arched an eyebrow. "Since when do you care?"

"Since you've gone and made this my case now. I'll have to write it up, won't I?"

Theo huffed a quiet laugh, some tension finally bleeding out of his chest.

"Don't die in there," Tucton said, more seriously this time.

"Would ruin your paperwork," Theo replied.

Tucton grinned. "Exactly."

With that, Theo gave him a curt nod and turned toward the tenement entrance. Behind him, he heard Tucton mutter: "Bloody madman."

"And you love me for it," Theo shot back over his shoulder.

He didn't glance back to check, but he knew Tucton would be moving. The man wasn't fool enough to wait around empty-handed. There was a police box two streets over, Theo could almost hear the hurried footsteps fading behind him. Backup would come, but too late. It had to be him, now. Alone.

Theo pressed on.

Ahead, the apartment block rose like a corpse of brick and stone. Once halfway decent, judging by the bones of its construction. Now it sagged in on itself. Boarded windows. Chipped paint. Ironwork bent at odd angles. The kind of place the council pretended didn't exist when journalists came sniffing.

As he reached the heavy door, it creaked open from the inside, ajar from years of abuse. A figure loomed in the dim, narrow space, a skinny young man in a threadbare jumper, sleeves pushed up, fingers scratching a raw patch on his forearm. The smell hit Theo immediately: damp, sweat, sour smoke, piss, and something acrid beneath it all.

The young man's eyes flitted up, wild and sunken. "Oi... you buying?" He fished in his pocket and produced two grubby wraps with trembling fingers. "Pure. Real stuff."

Theo brushed past without pause.

"Suit yourself," the dealer muttered, already turning back into the gloom.

Inside, the stairwell was steep and crooked. Crumbling plaster flaked from the walls. The banister was sticky to the touch, so Theo kept his hands clear. He moved quickly, boots light on rotting steps.

First floor.

The corridor yawned open, low ceilings, the space thick with heat and haze. Figures stood hunched against walls or slumped over broken chairs. No doors on the rooms anymore, just archways, makeshift curtains in tatters. Mattresses lay in piles, stained and lumpy, strewn with bottles, bent spoons, matches, bits of torn cloth.

A woman in a shapeless dress leaned out from a room, syringe hanging loose from her fingers. "Want a taste, love?" she rasped, voice dry as paper.

"No."

He pressed on. This was worse than he remembered. The place reeked of decay, not just of bodies, but of will, of hope.

As he climbed to the next landing, he spotted another pair, one sprawled across a sofa, one kneeling at their side, drawing a hit into thin arms. They didn't even look up as he passed. This wasn't the lively crash-spot of old. This was a mausoleum of addicts. The sense of time here had long since collapsed.

Second floor.

Fewer people here, but the rot had sunk in deeper. He stepped past a couple under a ragged blanket, rhythmic movement beneath. They didn't stop. Just paused to jab another hit mid-act. A sick mimicry of intimacy.

Theo moved on, fighting the churn in his gut.

Then, abrupt, someone stepped into his path.

Small, sharp-featured, hair hacked short, eyes glittering madly.

"Here," she giggled, thrusting a small pile of pills into his hand. "You look too bloody serious. Come on... lighten up."

Her palm pressed the capsules into his fingers. Theo caught them instinctively, reflex before thought.

And there they were.

Small, perfect, shining with promise.

How many nights had begun like this?

He could feel the pull already, the itch in the spine, the weight behind his eyes, the whisper: just one... what harm? Ease the ache. Loosen the fear.

The memories crashed forward, his first time, the soft spiral down, the borrowed warmth, the days lost in a fog that numbed every sharp edge. The comfort.

And now... here it was again. A hand's breadth away.

His fingers twitched.

Then another memory. Not comfort. Faces. Two faces.

Mother. Father.

And the blood that stained the walls of his past.

He closed his fist tight around the pills, then, slowly, with a sharp exhale, let them fall. They scattered across the floor, lost in the dirt and dust of the hallway.

He raised his gaze to the woman. "Not tonight."

And pushed past her.

20:31 16/03/1943 Whitton Road South Hounslow

Another flight up. His breath was rough now, his heart was hammering, from exertion aswell as the sense of wrongness building in his chest. Something coiled within his gut, a cold knot tightening with every step.

This floors landing was quieter.

Only two figures were visible, one sprawled inside a doorway to Theo's right, the other slumped over a chair at the end of the hallway. Both unmoving, passed out or worse, Theo didn't stop to check.

Far off, from the streets below, the sound of sirens grew closer, as if just outside the building. Tucton had successfully called for backup and it was coming fast.

Good, but it may be too late still.

Theo pressed onwards and upwards. another flight of stairs led him to a floor that was similar but shorter and thinner.

The noise from below dulled here, the drug haze thinned and doors... Every room on this floor had actual solid doors, made of wood, battered but intact.

That caught him. Odd.

He slowed, glancing up and down the corridor.

Every door was closed.

No movement.

No voices.

He reached for the first door, closest to him. It opened with a low groan. Inside, darkness, his eyes took a moment to adjust. When he could make out more that dark shapes, Theo's mouth dropped.

A pig.

Hung upside down.

Rope attaching its rear legs to the cieling.

It's throat was cut, clean and deep.

The floor beneath was covered in congealed black pools of rotting blood. The stench was rancid. Flies swarmed the room, filling Theo's ear with a buzzing that was ceaseless. Maggots writhed in the greying flesh.

The carcass was old, not new. It was possibly the first thing the Vampire killer practiced on.

Theo tried to lick his lips but his mouth was dry. He stepped back out of the room and closed the door behind him.

"Got to continue." Theo whispered to himself, grounding his thoughts, as he rested his hand on the second door.

The hinges groaned, resisting the motion.

The same smell from the first room greeting him again, this time his stomach threated to convulse.

This time however, a dog was hanging upside down from the cieling. A black Labrador, or what remained of one. The maggots had done a much better job at devouring this corpse.

Theo gagged and quickly shut the door.

This was no longer a crash spot for drug abusers, instead it had become the base of operations for the Vampire Killer.

Voices reached his ears, muffled by the distance, but it was clear the voices were authoritative. Tucton was advancing up the building.

So he continued, there was more to see here. He could feel it.

Theo rested his hand on the handle to door number three, and took a deep breath in, steadying himself incase a similar sight met him again.

The third door was heavier. Newer. Fitted tighter to its warped frame, as though meant to seal.

Theo pushed it open.

The room beyond wasn't like the others. Not at all.

Gone was the rot, the squalor, the stench. Here the air was cold, cleaner somehow, filtered through the soft mechanical hum of a fridge against the far wall. A makeshift lab, he realised at once. The centre of operations. The work of a precise, deliberate mind.

A large table dominated the room's heart, its surface scrubbed spotless, gleaming under the weak light of a single overhead bulb. Around it: stacked boxes of medical supplies, rows of glass jars, labelled with sharp, precise handwriting. Chemicals, solvents. Clean syringes in neat bundles. Scalpels laid in perfect order.

In the far corner, magazines, journals. Stacked high, some older, edges yellowed, others recent and sharp. All medical. Technical. Chemical sciences. Blood journals. Forensics. Anatomy.

Theo's pulse quickened.

Against the wall to the right, an upright cabinet, glass-fronted. Its contents displayed as though in some grim gallery. A plinth of sorts stood inside, shelves tiered in two neat rows. And there, spaced with the care of a collector: resin cubes.

Blood in every single one.

His breath caught.

Nine slots in total. All labelled. Theo predicted the first half of the labels. One slot for each murder scene.

The labels were just numbers, matching the ages of the victims. Starting with "75" on the left at the back and moving across to "35".

One slot, that was labelled "65", had been doubled up. His parents' cubes, unmistakable. Stacked on top of each other.

"35" was currently empty, that was the one that was left at the crime scene. Currently in evidence lockup. Accident? Maybe. But nothing here looked accidental. Every inch of this space was deliberate.

Then there was another empty slot, it was labelled "25". That was Alfie's.

That left three others.

Two were occupied. He leaned closer, eyes narrowing, the labels read:

"Mom" and "Dad".

Not a joint memorial, like the cube made for his own parents, a choice that echoed with meaning. Whoever had created these... they'd separated mother and father here. Unlike the forced pairing of Theo's own grief, frozen together in that sick memento. The killer's own family treated differently. Reverently.

A division of love, or pain? A line drawn between what was personal and what was performance?

His throat tightened.

The last space, empty, but prepared. A label already fixed beneath it.

"The happy couple."

Ice traced his spine.

If the killer was Maggie Shaw, if that piece of the puzzle was true, then what did this label mean? Was it him and Maggie? Had she planned him for this all along? But they'd only met a week ago. It didn't fit, unless someone else had been intended for this space before.

Theo reached out, fingers trembling slightly, and peeled the label back.

Slow, slow.

Beneath, a single word revealed itself:

Me.

Theo's breath locked.

A countdown. To suicide. Planned and prepared.

Why stop at fifteen? Was that age too low for her?

Were Children left untouched? Is that where the line is? A moral code, or an illusion of one? The contradictions twisted tighter, was this justice, madness, art? Who decided which lives were taken? Which spared?

Theo's mind raced, but now wasn't the time.

Al and Maggie were here somewhere. That much he knew now with certainty.

And if he didn't find them soon, he'd be too late.

12. OLD FRIENDS
21:21 16/03/1943
Whitton Road South Hounslow

Theo found the door.

No logic to it, his mind wasn't working like that anymore. No deduction. Just... gravity. Something pulling him to this spot. A simple wooden door, worn at the edges, scuffed from years of uncaring use.

He pressed his palm flat to it. Cold.

Then, without thought, without breath, he pushed it open.

The world beyond felt muffled, air thick with something unseen. A single bare bulb hummed faintly overhead, the light pooling in a sickly halo on the cracked floorboards.

She was there.

Maggie.

Kneeling, back slightly hunched, her hair loose in strands around her face. In her hands, a length of coarse rope, moving steadily through her fingers. Her touch was gentle. Intent. She was binding ankles, tying the rope neatly, as if this were no more than ordinary work.

Al.

Limp. Slumped awkwardly, arms hanging. Rope burns circled his wrists. His face, pale, slack-jawed. No fight left in him. Barely breathing.

Theo stood frozen in the doorway.

"Maggie..." His voice came out wrong. Hollow.

She looked up, slowly. No surprise in her face. No fear. Just... quiet recognition.

"You came," she said softly.

Theo's hands twitched at his sides. The words stuck in his throat. Every part of him, heart, mind, breath, locked in place.

"Let him go," he forced out, the sound thin, frayed at the edges.

Maggie rose to stand, not hurried, not defensive. Calm. Like they were two old friends in conversation.

"I knew you'd come," she said. Her smile... small. Almost warm.

"Why?" Theo's breath caught. His chest ached. "Why are you doing this?"

She tilted her head. "You don't remember me."

His mind snagged on that, trying to grasp the meaning.

"I was there," she went on, voice gentle as if soothing a child. "A long time ago. You wouldn't know it, you were too far gone. You shared with me. On that floor... do you remember? You told me what it was like. To have a mind that never rests."

Theo's pulse pounded in his ears.

She took a small step forward. Her voice dropped, more intimate now:

"You said... you wished it would slow. Just for a moment. That you wished you could breathe."

A faint image, flickering, half-formed. A room, a floor, blurred voices. A stranger's hand. Comfort? He couldn't be sure. His mind refused to settle.

"I needed to give you something," Maggie whispered. "A

puzzle. Something worthy of you."

Theo shook his head, the words barely reaching him.

"I never wanted this," he managed. "This isn't..."

"It was beautiful," she said, her voice trembling now. "Watching you work. Seeing what you became. The first murder, as perfect as it was, only caught the attention of the police, I needed something bigger. So, when I, when I..."

She faltered. The smile faded. Tears threatened to fall from the edges of her eyes.

"My parents," Theo whispered. His mind went blank.

Maggie's breath caught. "That was when you changed. You became... alive."

Pain bloomed sharp in Theo's chest. His throat closed around the grief rising there.

"You killed them." Theo flinched, surprised at how loud he had spoken.

Tear began to fall from her eyes. "Yes, I love you. I love your mind. You gave me a chance to be free, so I returned the favour."

A silence stretched between them, thick, suffocating.

Theo's mind reeled. The betrayal, deeper than logic, deeper than words.

"Why?" he rasped.

She looked down at the rope in her hands, fingers flexing gently.

"To see you. To see what you truly are. You didn't disappoint. You have become the best detective in Hounslow, London, possibly the world."

Maggie's fingers moved almost absently, caressing the worn rope.

Theo's gaze dropped to Al, his limbs slack, skin sallow. The breath hitching shallow in his chest. Barely alive. No awareness. No resistance.

His voice broke, more air than words: "You don't have to do this."

She lifted her gaze again, softer now. And so... tired. The sparkle that had danced in her eyes that first day in the coffee shop, gone. What remained was weary devotion. A devotion that chilled him to his bones.

"I have to," she said simply. "It has to end. For both of us."

Theo's fists curled, nails biting into his palms. He stepped closer, slow, deliberate, as if movement itself required permission.

"You've done enough," he said quietly. "You've shown me everything. You've already changed me."

Maggie's smile flickered. A small, fragile thing.

"I hated it, y'know," she said. Her voice trembled. "I hated every one of them. But after... after your parents... I couldn't stop."

"You hated it because it was unnecessary."

"Each kill has been necessary to your recovery, all of it was necessary to rise you up above all others."

"Even the couple that you stole the drugs from?"

A single tear fell from Maggie's eye, "Yes, unfortunately, yes. Even my closest friends. I needed more drugs desperately, my time was running out."

"Why Maggie?" A sinking feeling was intensifying within his chest, his heart was falling, despite knowing it was physically impossible, it was how he felt, and he couldn't explain it.

"Because you... you were brilliant. Watching you, your mind, your grief, your fire... I couldn't stop."

Theo swallowed hard. His throat burned with unshed grief.

His mind, usually so sharp, felt sluggish, caught between rage, sorrow, guilt.

"You watched me," he whispered.

"For years," Maggie breathed. "I tried to come back to you. To talk to you. I tried to be what you needed."

Her eyes shimmered with tears now.

"The officer. The nurse. The woman in the café who didn't care. None of it worked. Until..."

She gestured vaguely, her hands trembling now.

"Until you were alone enough to see me."

Theo's breath caught again, his body frozen in the thick, cloying air of the room.

"And the cubes," he rasped. "The resin. Why?"

Maggie's eyes brightened faintly, like a child eager to show a drawing.

"For you," she whispered. " Something the others couldn't understand. So, they would need you. So, you would feel needed. It was all part of the show."

"So why are we both in the last slot? was this going to end in a double suicide? You're not thinking straight anymore. The killing has warped your mind."

"I see clearly. We are in love, we will live together forever, die together."

"You are not making sense."

She reached down again, gripping the rope that fed up through the pulley.

Theo's heart lurched. "Maggie..."

"It's the last," she said softly. "After this, it ends."

Her hand pulled, slow, steady.

Al's body jerked, lifted inch by inch from the floor. His arms dangled limp at his sides, head tilting forward, chin to chest. Drool glistened at the corner of his mouth.

Theo's chest seized. The room seemed to tilt. His feet were stuck to the spot. He urged his legs to move forwards but they threated to buckle at any moment.

"Stop," he said, louder this time. "You can still choose. You don't have to..."

Maggie's grip tightened on the rope.

"I do."

Her other hand, slipping now into her coat, drew out a blade. Thin, sharp, gleaming under the single naked bulb.

Theo's world narrowed.

"Please," he said, his voice raw. "If you loved me. Then hear me now: you don't have to do this."

Maggie's gaze locked onto his, filled with a heart-breaking, terrible affection.

"I'm doing it for you," she whispered.

And she moved.

"NO!" Theo screamed.

He surged forward, but the blade was already rising,

The blade arced down, fast, practised.

Theo's foot caught on the edge of a loose board, his hand reaching, but too late.

Maggie's pull on the rope slipped at the same moment the knife came down. The rig, imperfect under strain, gave way, Al's body dropped suddenly, twisting mid-air,

A sickening crack of bone against timber.

Theo flinched. His breath caught.

The knife had sliced wide, not across the throat as intended, but low, slashing deep across Al's stomach as the body crumpled onto the floor.

The impact jarred the room.

For one long moment, neither of them moved.

Theo's gaze locked on Al, on the ragged tear in his abdomen, the grotesque spilling of viscera across the dusty boards. Blood, dark and pooling, crept outward in slow rivulets. Steam rose faintly in the chill air.

The only sound now, wet, sickening, the sluggish ooze of life spilling out.

Theo's pulse hammered behind his eyes. His stomach knotted. Bile threatened.

He couldn't move.

Maggie stood frozen too, knife still gripped in a trembling fist. Her chest rose and fell unevenly. She stared down at Al's broken body, expression unreadable, caught somewhere between grief and grim resolve.

The spell of silence broke, the door to the room crashed open. Theo whipped his head round.

Tucton.

Maggie's eyes widened.

She pivoted, too fast, knife gleaming.

Theo stumbled back, dropping into a half-stance, ready, heart racing. His mind screamed do something, but his limbs felt heavy, slow, dragged down by shock, grief, the weight of everything unspoken.

Maggie came at him again, knife out, her steps wild, grief-fuelled,

CRACK.

A single shot.

Maggie's body jerked, shoulder spinning, her momentum

faltering.

She slipped, legs sliding out beneath her on the wet boards,

And fell hard, landing face-first with a dull thud.

The room rang with silence again.

Theo barely breathed.

Tucton's voice barked from the door: "Stay back!"

But Theo was already moving, slow, wary, toward her crumpled form.

Blood seeped beneath her from the wound, but she wasn't dead. Her fingers twitched weakly.

He knelt beside her, turning her gently,

And saw her smile. Faint. Tired.

The knife, gone from her hand. Embedded deep in her own stomach.

Her hand fluttered upward, seeking.

Theo sank to his knees fully, throat tight. One tear slipped free, tracing the line of his jaw.

Her fingertips brushed his cheek wiping the tear away in the process.

Voice thin, trembling with fading breath:

"I did it... for you..."

Theo swallowed hard, every emotion warring inside, guilt, sorrow, strange tenderness.

Then quietly Theo leaned in and whispered,

"I know, Thankyou... I loved you."

A cough, a wet, ragged sound.

"I love you too..."

Her hand fell away. Her eyes fluttered closed, still smiling faintly.

Theo leaned down, forehead to hers, holding there, waiting... until the faint rise of her chest ceased.

Still.

Gone.

He let out a long, trembling breath.

Gently, reverently, he laid her head back against the floor. Smoothed her hair once.

He rose slowly, adjusting his coat with trembling fingers. There was no need for words.

Without looking back, Theo walked to where Tucton stood. They faced each other in the dim light, the noise of the corridor falling away.

In a quiet moment of understanding, each man placed a hand on the other's shoulder. The grip held for a breath, maybe two, neither of them in a hurry to let go.

Theo met Tucton's eyes. His own vision shimmered, tears gathering at the corners. When the blur became too much, he released his hold.

With a small nod, he turned and walked past the gathered officers. Tucton's voice cut through the silence, ordering them to make way.

Theo stepped out into the cold night air. And went home.

13. MOVING FORWARD

8:00 12/06/1943
17 Ellington Road East Hounslow

Morning light streams weakly through the half-drawn curtains. The kitchen is warm with the familiar clink of mugs and the scent of strong tea.

Theo padded into the room, coat slung over one shoulder, still fastening the cuffs of his shirt. The weariness in his eyes was less visible today, replaced by something quieter. Settled.

At the table, Darrell sat already, two plates in front of him, tea steaming in mismatched cups. Toast stacked in neat triangles.

"You're early," Theo remarked, setting his coat on the back of the chair.

Darrell smiled, not his usual dry smirk, but something softer. "It's the day, isn't it?"

Theo pulled out the chair, sat. Reached for a slice of toast. "It is."

Darrell watched him carefully. "How do you feel?"

Theo thought about lying. Instead, he chewed, swallowed, and said simply, "Ready."

A pause, just long enough to be noticed.

"You sure?" Darrell pressed, voice dropping.

Theo met his gaze. "I've let too much of the past drive me. But today, I take it back. That includes Alfie."

Another silence. Darrell looked down at the tea, then back. "And Maggie?"

Theo's jaw tightened, but only slightly. "She's somewhere better."

He didn't say the rest: Better to remember her as Mags, not the Vampire Killer. The first woman he ever...

He wouldn't give the thought air.

He took another bite of toast instead, letting the act settle the room.

Darrell gave a small, pitiful smile. "Good. You're... different."

Theo nodded once, finishing his tea in a single long pull. He rose, moved to the mirror above the mantle.

A small ritual. Tie straightened. Hair in place. Jacket smoothed. The reflection stared back, tired but composed.

"It's my first day back," he said aloud, voice carrying a little weight. "Radcliffe agreed, pending tests. Tucton... put in a good word. I always thought of him as another beat cop, but he earned my respect that night. Few do."

Darrell gave a short laugh. "Well, I'll be damned."

Theo grabbed his coat from the chair.

"Thanks," he said. Not just for breakfast. For all of it.

Darrell gave him a nod, eyes bright despite the hour.

Theo moved to the door, pulled it open.

"You'll do fine," Darrell called after him. "You always do."

Theo didn't turn. He simply stepped out into the crisp air, hands in his pockets, shoulders squared. No backward glance. No hesitation.

A new day.

A new chapter.

ABOUT THE AUTHOR

Ashley Carvel

Ashley has always been drawn to the concept of solving through deductions. Sherlock Holmes, Bones, Elementary, House and NAtional Treasure. People who are considered too different for society actual being the most observant person in the room.

Their love for Detective Thrillers and immersive storytelling led them to craft the story of Theodore Nash. A Consultant, working with the police, using his skills of deduction, Misdirection and working in the Grey area of the law.

This series is dedicated to my wife, who has saved my life, not once, but twice.

Ashley also created - "The Conductor's Paradox" Series, "The God-Touched Saga" and the "Arlo Fenn" Novels.

☐ Follow Ashley Carvel on:
Facebook: Ashley Carvel Novels
Instagram: @BloodLustAsh
TikTok: Ashley Carvel Novels @BloodLustAsh
Youtube: @AshleyCarvelNovels

BOOKS BY THIS AUTHOR

Divine Awakening

Divine Ascension

Divine Ruin

The Conductors Paradox (Books 1-4)

Criminally Tender

Printed in Dunstable, United Kingdom